AN INDIAN FARRAGO

Stories and Poems

MOHIT KHARE

Leadstart
INKSTATE

ISBN 978-93-5458-231-8

First published in India 2021 by Leadstart Inkstate
A brand of One Point Six Technologies Pvt. Ltd.

123, Building J2, Shram Seva Premises,
Wadala Truck Terminal,
Mumbai 400022, Maharashtra, INDIA
Phone: +91 96999 33000
Email: info@leadstartcorp.com
www.leadstartcorp.com

Disclaimer: This is a work of fiction. All the names, characters, businesses, places, events and incidents in this book are either the product of the author's imagination or used in a fictitious manner. Any resemblance to actual persons, living or dead, or actual events is purely coincidental.

Editor: Vaibhav Pathare
Cover: Swapnil Behere
Layouts: Kshitij Dhawale

For my parents

About the Author

Mohit Khare is a financial services technology professional who has worked with various multinational IT and banking firms. He holds a Master's in Business Administration from the University of Lucknow and currently works as a Product Manager with one of the largest banks in the world. He currently lives in Mumbai with his wife and son.

The writer's bug bit him when he was in college. What started as outpourings to provide solace against the pangs of heartbreak, soon turned into a keen interest in writing stories and poems inspired by what he saw and felt. His early writings, few poems followed by articles, featured in one of India's leading newspapers, The Times of India, Lucknow edition, providing the adrenalin rush to continue his creative pursuits.

While he completed his higher education and subsequently traversed the corporate world making a career in information technology, Mohit continued to write, filling up the closet with short stories and poems. He completed a Diploma in Scriptwriting in 2016 from Writer Prepares, Mumbai, to marry his passion for writing and movies. Mohit is also a member of

The Screenwriters Association of India. He is credited as the associate scriptwriter for few episodes of an Indian television series called "Khwaabon Ki Zamin Par" that was aired on Zindagi channel in 2016.

In his spare time off work, Mohit continues to write both in English and Hindi and also loves to indulge in developing ideas for scripts for feature films.

This is his first book.

https://mohitkhare.in/

ACKNOWLEDGEMENTS

Whether a writer is born or made can be a matter of great intellectual debate. But none can contest the fact that writers are shaped each passing day of their lives. The experiences of life mold them constantly.

As with each great structure, this mold is supported by pillars around it which ensures its strength and stability as it grows. For me, as would be for many, these pillars have been the unflinching love and support of family and friends. It is a matter of pride for me to acknowledge their efforts in shaping up my life not only as an author but more so as a human being.

It all starts with my parents, Sheela and Ram Chandra Khare, who have always let me do what I wanted to in life. They always strived to provide me with the best in life, many times at the expense of cutting down on their own needs. Thank you Mummy and Papa for all your love and blessings.

A heartfelt thanks to my wife, Anjana, for being a supporting rock in my life. A dreamer and thinker like me needed to have such a quintessential anchor behind him.

My son Evyavan, who keeps us going, supporting us in his own little ways. In him I see myself growing up. He is as excited as I am to have my work see the light of the day.

I am blessed to have some great relatives who have constantly provided me with support and love. A sincere thanks to all of them as well.

Friends support you as no one does, but it would be impossible to list all their names here. Starting from school, college and university friends in Lucknow, to the colleagues in Delhi, Mumbai, and Tokyo, if you are reading this, know that I truly value and appreciate all that you have given to me through our relationship.

And lastly, a big thank you to you, dear reader, for entrusting me with a few precious hours from your life. I hope you like the book.

Introduction

I don't remember writing anything creatively worthwhile till my high school. But I read a lot, experimented with a wide variety of subjects and authors. Things changed in grade 11. I suddenly found myself capable of writing poetry. Whether it was the gush of the arrival of youth or the fruition of my pursuit for reading, I am uncertain, but they just kept coming. When two of these poems made it to the Young Talent column in The Times of India, Lucknow edition, it was a proud moment for me. I realized that apart providing immense satisfaction, writing made me new friends in my college. Soon, I started keeping a diary which was to become a true friend in the years to come.

I turned to prose and a few articles out of the ones I wrote made their way to the newspaper again. This time it made my parents proud as one of them was about our golden days in the desert region of Rajasthan. I got my first cheque, of a hundred rupees, for that article, a moment which I cherish till date, not for the money but for the sense of achievement it brought.

For a young guy, for whom writing was just a hobby, this was a major pat on the back, and so I made it a point to keep writing. My diary kept me busy, but I realized I had to give a different shape to my thoughts that emanated from meeting diverse people and having myriad experiences in life. And thus was born the first short story, and then another and another. I kept writing them over the years, never thinking about getting them published. For me, the high point had already been reached, credits as a writer in the newspaper and anything other than that was a dream.

Cut to the year 2016 and I found my name flashing on the television screen with credits in the writing department for a television series. I had found a new love, film/tv scripts. While it's still early days for me in this arena but my little successes give me hope. I am glad that I kept my interest in writing alive and kicking while climbing the ladders in the corporate world in my day job.

While I was busy romancing my scripts these past few years, I conveniently ignored the closet brimming with my other writings. Until recently, when the closet broke open and all the short stories and poems marched out, crying foul, demanding due justice to my first labours of love. The want was justified and timely, so here I am presenting them in front of you.

These stories and poems have been written over the years, some of them over two decades ago and some as fresh as the last year. I have carefully selected 12 stories and 12 poems from my treasure trove. Some of these are thought-provoking and poignant, while some sparkling with fun or resonating with warmth, but all adding diversity to the farrago called life.

CONTENTS

Every Story is Us

- Rumi

Stories

1

GATTU

Shahzaada ran briskly, springing in between like an antelope, his nose high in the air. He sniffed trouble; he was not sure what it was but his god-gifted sense told him something was wrong.

He paused at the roundabout amid the shanties, where Gattu used to play with the children living in the slum. Shahzaada looked around. As expected, he did not find Gattu there. Shahzaada quickened his pace and moved ahead, continuing his search. It had rained heavily for the last couple of days and his paws were sordid with mud and dirt. The slums were flooded, at some places with knee-deep water, and he had to jump and crisscross to maintain his speed.

Gattu had been with him for the last two days. It had rained so heavily that they had to leave their shelter near Munna Bhai's tea stall and move in the courtyard of the locality's temple. The priest had reprimanded Gattu many times not to bring his dog inside the temple premises but Gattu had sneaked in Shahzaada as soon as the priest fled away to his home a day before, due to the incessant rains. Shahzaada remembered Gattu hugging him and muttering the previous night, "What problem does that pujari have in allowing you in? You are better off than many of those who pray here each morning, almost bringing down the temple bells and do all types of inhuman activities for the rest of the day!". That was the last time he had received a hug from Gattu and then they had dozed off.

Shahzaada couldn't remember when Gattu left in the morning. He had waited for some time for Gattu to return. He could see that the temple had been surrounded by water. He had never seen such incessant rain in his life. The downpour had lashed the city continuously for the last two days and he could see the effect it had on the slum. It had stopped raining in the morning and people were coming out of their houses and huts. There was muck floating all around. He had seen Munna glancing blindly at his tea stall, which was flooded with water. The awning over the entrance of his shop was in tatters and many of his tea glasses and plates had fallen to the ground either soiled or broken. The bench where people used to sit to drink tea and which served as Gattu's bed in the night, was however intact. Shahzaada raised his head and looked around some more. The children of the slum, bored of staying inside their houses had been let free by the harried parents. They were running amok amidst all the people around, splashing in the water and shoving mud at each other. They added the only spark of mirth to the otherwise gloomy scene around. From the temple courtyard, Shahzaada could see people rushing here and there, umbrellas in their hand, ready to face the day, lest the heavens poured again. Shahzaada wondered why the temple was still deserted today. By this time of the day usually, the temple was busy with people pushing and shoving each other to reach the deity and get blessings from the priest. Today incidentally even he had not turned up and the gates to the deity were still locked. "Didn't anyone need blessings today? These humans are strange!", Shahzaada thought.

But he knew that there were some good ones around too. The two he was in love with immensely were Gattu and Rehman chacha. Now over three years old, sturdily built, white and brown Indian Pariah with a stiff high tail, Shahzaada had been raised since birth by Gattu. Gattu on the other hand largely had been raised by Rehman chacha, the taxi driver, and Munna bhaiya, the tea stall owner. Not that either of the two had adopted him, but because most of his needs for clothing, food, and shelter were catered courtesy of those two. Apart from necessities, there was more that they had given to Gattu and that was warmth and love, a hard thing to find for an orphan growing up in one of the many bustling slums in the city. And Gattu had given that same amount of love in turn to Shahzaada treating him more like a friend than a pet.

He waited for Gattu in the temple courtyard for a bit more. Maybe he had gone to get something to eat for them. Shahzaada knew that Gattu would remember that they had not eaten the last night and that he was starved. He was sure Gattu would manage something, as always. Gattu had always scolded Shahzaada when he tried to eat leftovers from the dustbins or something strewn on the streets. Gattu's multiple reprimands on the subject had resulted in a habit and Shahzaada never touched any such thing. He would always wait for Gattu to bring him his food. Shahzaada knew Gattu loved him dearly. Often at nights when they sat alone together on the bench at Munna's tea stall, Gattu would talk to Shahzaada and tell him things, some of which he understood and some which he didn't. But he liked it immensely when they sat together like that, Gattu stroking his head softly, tickling his neck, patting his back, and talking more to himself rather than to Shahzaada.

One of the things which Gattu often repeated was how Shahzaada got his name. "You know, everyone around including Pappu, Ravi, Golu, all suggested me to keep your name like Jackie, Tommy, etc. What rubbish, I didn't like any one of those at all, are these names suitable for a handsome dog like you? Sounds more like actors from those action-packed foreign films. Even Munna bhaiya gave such a pathetic name, Moti. I even called you that for a few days", Gattu said laughing. "But I didn't like it a bit. Then one day I told this to Rehman chacha. He asked me; 'Tell me what this small puppy means to you'. I could not answer. I said I love him. Rehman chacha just laughed. Then he turned on the TV, and Chachi brought us some tea. Chacha started pondering over my request. He sipped the tea and started focusing on the movie running on the TV channel. 'Mughal-e-Azam, what a film, watch this Gattu', he told me, and the two of us started concentrating on the movie. I heard an elderly actor roar in a heavy voice 'Shahzaade, tum hume aziz ho'. I was impressed by the dialogue but didn't understand much. I asked Rehman chacha what that meant. Rehman chacha told me that the old man is trying to say that the hero is dear to him. 'So is the hero's name Shahzaade?', I enquired. Rehman chacha smiled and told me that Shahzaada meant prince. The old man in the movie was a king and the other one the prince, and the old man loved him dearly. Suddenly I was struck by an idea. 'Chacha I got a new name for Moti'. Rehman chacha looked back at me surprised at first and then smiled back convincingly, 'Shazaada, what a fine name!'".

Hashib-ur-Rehman or Rehman chacha, as everyone in the

neighbourhood called him, had been living in the slums for over two decades now. He had come to Mumbai from northern India in search of a job. A post-graduate in arts and a pious human being, he soon got dismayed by the gloomy opportunities and settled for driving a taxi to earn his living. Now, twenty years later he had taxis that he owned, one of which he ran himself and the others were leased out. His was one of the only few fully constructed concrete and brick house amongst a din of makeshift dwellings in the slum. He now earned a decent living to support his small family comprising a wife and a school-going son.

Rehman had known Gattu since his childhood. Nobody knew much about Gattu's family. His mother had come to the slums with him when he was merely seven years old. She had rented a small hut from Munna. Nobody knew where she had come from. She barely spoke about herself but had developed good relations with Rehman and Munna's wives. She had started working as a housemaid in a few homes in the nearby residential complexes. She suddenly passed away one day, complaining of high fever and pain. It later came out that she was seeing some doctor in the neighbourhood slums and supposedly had a serious case of Jaundice. Nobody ever knew much about her or her illness. After she passed away there was no one to take care of Gattu. Munna had no choice but to rent out the hut to someone else and Gattu was left to the mercy of Munna and Rehman's families' support.

Rehman had been having a bad day at work. It had been raining heavily and he had not earned much. The passengers were fewer to find and many a time his old cab also fell prey to wading waters, getting stuck now and then. He had decided to ferry only short-distance passengers around his area for the last two days. He was astonished to see the amount of water building up on the roads. He felt bad each time he said no to a distressed passenger but he had to politely refuse. It made no sense to put his old cab through such suffering. Just the other day he had seen a young lady getting drenched in the heavy rainfall. He could see several cabs decline to attend to her. He had almost finished his day and was planning to return home. Seeing the woman in distress he agreed to go in the opposite direction only to be first stuck in heavy traffic and later having an axle broken down due to an open pothole on a water peddled road. He received his usual fare and a seemingly grateful "thanks" in return. As it turned out later, the cost of the repair itself surpassed the fare he had earned from the lady that day.

Shahzaada had now looked around all the places within the locality where he hoped to find Gattu. There was no trace of him. Shahzaada felt afraid now. He did not know what to do next. And he was hungry too. He walked towards Munna Bhai's shop to check on him. Since the rain had stopped Munna was at his stall cleaning up the mess around. Shahzaada walked over and slid under the bench where he used to sleep when Gattu retired for the day on the bench.

He was saddened and let out a small wail, loud enough for Munna to hear. "Shazaada, are you here?" he inquired. "Come on boy, come to me", he called out. Shahzaada came out and wagged his tail lovingly at Munna. "Where's Gattu? How come he's not with you?", Munna was puzzled. Shahzaada moved closer to Munna who patted him lovingly. He pulled out a packet of biscuits from his stall's cabinet and dished out a few to the dog, who gobbled them up greedily. His hunger satiated, Shahzaada hid under the bench again for some rest.

How and when Manish Kumar came to be popularly called Munna, nobody knew, but he remembered people calling him so ever since he was a young lad. When he opened his tea stall in the slums ten years ago, he acknowledged the name his admirers had given him by aptly naming it Munna Bhai's tea corner. Now all at 40, Munna was doing relatively well. His tea stall had grown to a small eatery, providing cheap breakfast, affordable lunch, evening snacks, and dinner to those residing around and working their lives out to earn their living in the busy metropolis. Of course, after all these years the hottest selling item in his shop remained the hot tea.

Munna was married but had no children. Both he and his wife were very fond of Gattu. Ever since his arrival into the area, they had been a part of his growing up. They had helped him with food, shelter, and clothing with generous help and contribution from Rehman chacha. Gattu felt the same way about both families. Somehow, they made up a bit for the parents he never had.

Shahzaada was soon on his feet again to continue his search for Gattu. He had already searched all the places in the vicinity where they lived, where Gattu could be usually found. Shahzaada knew he would now need to go out of the slum area onto the main road towards the highway where Gattu might be found, manning the traffic signal.

Gattu had this habit to help people in whatever small way he could, in whatever manner his childish and uneducated thinking would tell him to. The elders in the shanty loved him as he helped them carry the groceries home, the mothers and housewives loved him as he would run errands for them, when they were busy, without batting an eyelid or expecting anything in return. All this, while the lads of his age were busy playing cricket, emulating Bollywood stars, gossiping, and even fighting with each other. Gattu felt good if he got a pat on the back or a hug for what he did for others. He felt a part of them then. A few years ago, when he was running one such errand for Munna Bhai's wife, to bring a detergent soap from the grocery store, he went to the shop on the main street outside the slum area. Gattu had noticed that the shopkeeper at the main road usually gave items for lesser prices than those within the slum. While returning he witnessed traffic chaos at the junction on the main road leading to the highway and people honking and shouting from inside their vehicles. He also saw a couple of men trying to help to ease the jam in absence of any police officers around. Gattu too volunteered and took up one end of the tri-section. He followed the people at the other two points and started stopping and signalling people according to their directives. He found it difficult at first with many not heeding his calls due to his age and size. However, with the help of the other two who intervened intermittently at Gattu's end too, he was successfully able to hold his position and help clear the traffic jam. Gattu felt happy that day. He did get a chiding from Munna Bhai's wife for being late with the detergent soap, but he found a new activity for himself to while away some amount of time from his day.

Gattu started putting around three to four hours per day on that traffic signal. He quickly identified the peak rush hours and made it a point to reach the junction at those times. He worked with different people, many times helping commoners and at other times with police officers.

At first, a few of the police officers beat him and husked him off telling him it's not his job to man crossings. But they soon realized that in the utter chaos on the road a helping hand did not harm and sometimes also proved useful to take long breaks away from duty. Gattu soon became a fixture in the rush hours at that crossing. Although the police officers who were manning the traffic changed sometimes, two or three faces were usually always present with him during rush hours. He had grown to know most of them over time.

There was Atmaram who was aged, bulging, and almost ready for retirement. Atmaram was laid back and a lazy policeman and Gattu always wondered whether he didn't like to work or didn't want to. Atmaram was often missing from action and Gattu had noted that his presence, rather than being a help to others, created more confusion.

Gattu remembered when Atmaram had almost caused accidents by releasing the wrong side of the traffic in total disregard of the directives from the other sides and even the automated signal, which like Atmaram was rarely working. Rather than being apologetic about his behaviour he had beaten both Gattu and a poor motorcycle driver who had almost missed hitting people coming from the other side due to the ruckus. Gattu didn't like him much.

The other two policemen posted at the crossing were much younger, sensible, and dedicated. One was named Prakash and the other was called JP. Gattu didn't know till now what the name JP stood for. JP held the traffic at the end farthest from

Gattu. So, he didn't have much interaction with him. But he knew Prakash very well, as he manned a part of the same end that Prakash managed. Gattu liked Prakash. He was a young man, in his late twenties, very dedicated to whatever he did. Gattu liked him because he always reached on time, didn't take many breaks, and was always smiling and talking to people around. Gattu liked his style of working, never arguing with people on the street or those driving vehicles, never bossing around but rather behaving pleasantly with them and helping them. Gattu called him "Parkas Bhai" (somehow, he found his name too complex for his tongue).

Prakash on some days offered Gattu to join him for tea, after his duty hours at that crossing was over. When they sat together initially, Prakash talked about general things but after a few days, he started opening up and telling about himself. He would sometimes talk at length about his lonely life in Mumbai away from his parents in Ratnagiri. He would talk about his plans to make a name for himself in the police force, to do something big. At other times he talked about his plans for marriage. When he would finish, he would stare at Gattu to gauge how much he had understood. Gattu even with his limited understanding of the world realized that perhaps Prakash just needed someone to vent out his feelings.

In one such discussion, Prakash asked Gattu, "What do you want to become when you grow up?". Gattu thought for a while and said, "Be a policeman, like you!". Prakash laughed, "You are already one. You do half my work", he said patting him on the back. Gattu smiled sheepishly, "But I don't have a uniform!".

Prakash got him a policeman's dress, available for kids at the local store nearby, the very next day. Gattu felt elated. For him, it was almost being inducted into the police force. The dress did wonders to his confidence and he became more dedicated to his part-time job of managing traffic.

The dress became the talk of his slum area for the initial few days. Most of the children who did not get along with Gattu teased him by calling him a fake policewala. They would make noises like the police siren when he passed by. Some of them stood up and performed animated gestures either saluting him or copying the traffic policemen's actions.

However, some others were pleased with this development as well. That dress got Gattu his first set of real friends amongst the boys in the vicinity who were drawn to him because of his proximity with the policemen. The elders and women in the locality praised Gattu for his good work. The dress also got Gattu a few admirers in the girls of his age in the shanties. They would blush and giggle in a group when Gattu passed by flaunting his new dress on way to work, his chest protruded and his lips curving into a thin smile sensing the girls' presence.

Gattu had hugged Shahzaada almost to suffocation when he wore that dress on the first day. When he returned from work that day, he hugged him again and told him about the dress and the impression it had created.

It was that same khaki dress that Shahzaada searched for now, as he hit the main road in search of Gattu. The downpour had increased and streets had started flooding. Shahzaada wondered where all the rain was coming from since the last few days. He was perplexed why Gattu had ventured out in this weather. He was drenched now. He stopped at the entrance of the slum where the main road appeared. He shook his body to wriggle his coat and glanced around quickly. No trace of Gattu still. He knew he would need to go further till the highway where Gattu went for managing the traffic. An instinct in him knew it was dangerous to venture out with so much water around in the streets. Another thing that he was apprehensive about was leaving his territory and entering another. Although he was a sturdily built handsome dog, Shahzaada knew that trespassing into other dogs' territory meant trouble, he could easily be outnumbered.

Wriggling his coat once again he paused for one more moment, then Gattu's love drove him against his instincts and he started running towards the highway tearing through the sea of humans and automobiles, braving the gushing water on the road.

It had been raining very heavily in Mumbai that day, more than anyone had expected, or anyone had witnessed in the past. Without any warning, the city had started to flood and people were in a panic. All the offices, shops, and other working establishments closed early in the afternoon that day and people rushed in a mad spree to reach home safely. For some, it was a timely decision, but for most, it was too late. Thousands were marooned on way to their home, stranded in water-logged areas. The flooding water was everywhere, on the streets, inside low-lying homes, and in the slums, wreaking havoc. At some places, the water ran so deep on the streets that people had to form human chains and cling to each other to escape its fury and force. The local trains were stranded, buses fought to keep their engines alive in half-drowned conditions, and cars could be seen floating on the roads at the push of a hand in the mayhem.

In Gattu's slum, the water started rushing into homes. The garbage-filled drains took no time in overflowing and added to the chaos. Munna was aghast as his tea and sugar containers were snatched away by the flowing water. The water's speed and depth were increasing by the hour and Munna had to transport all his shop's goods to his home and keep it on top of the cupboards. He was worried as the water was eating into the semi-solid foundation of the awnings over his tea stall.

In another part of the city Rehman was busy faring troubled passengers to their destination by his taxi, never thinking about (unlike most other drivers) which direction or route they wanted him to go. His experience in the city told him that things were in a bad shape and that this was not just an ordinary monsoon day. He could sense further trouble brewing. He had decided to run his taxi till he could do it today. He had just ferried back six panic-stricken school students to their parents, whose gratitude had filled his day with warmth. He was now ferrying an old couple home. He could see people stranded and wading through knee-deep water at most places. His old Fiat was behaving bravely till now, never complaining, but as they got closer to the old couple's home, the engine started giving in. The water level was higher there and Rehman knew it would be difficult to go ahead. "We are just about half a kilometre away", the old man pleaded. Rehman knew that if he tried to go ahead there was a risk of the taxi breaking down. "Is there no alternate way? The water level is rising, the taxi will stop midway". The old man sighed heavily, "No this is the only way". Rehman knew it would be unethical to let the old passengers out in the open to fend for themselves through the flooded street. He looked to the heavens for support and plunged his vehicle ahead. What he feared though came true just a few meters away. The taxi stopped and wouldn't start again. He couldn't blame anyone. The old lady seemed terrified. Rehman had no choice but to get out of the taxi. The water was almost entering through the doors of the cab now. The old man followed him and stumbled adjusting to the current. "She would not be able to walk in this flow", he commented, balancing himself and pointing to his wife, the old lady. Rehman felt helpless. "What shall we do?", the old man blurted out a question pointed to no one in particular. "Get inside, please", Rehman told him, "I will try and get some help". He waded his way through the water towards the side of the road where he could see some men standing beside the closed shop and stalls.

He implored them to push the taxi with him, explaining the plight of the couple inside it. Two of them came for help and soon some other good samaritans joined in. Surprisingly the taxi felt much lighter due to the rising water and increasing flow. Nature's fury helped the poor old couple reach near their apartment from where they climbed the footpath and walked home, clutching the railings and boundary walls around. Rehman's taxi did not start. He had no choice but to lock it and leave it beside the roadside near the old couple's house. He would have felt concerned to leave it unattended this way any other day. But today was different. Today it was just another vehicle adding to the plethora of stranded and abandoned vehicles that filled up the streets. He had to walk a long way before he came across a known taxi driver who later dropped him home.

Gattu was missing since morning and Shahzaada was now worried as it was now few hours past noon. The clouds above had not relented and the downpour continued its wrathful form. Shahzaada sped towards the highway where Gattu usually helped the policemen control the traffic. As he reached near the highway, he felt the water getting deeper and his balance wavering. He could feel the current thumping stronger against his chest. A few steps ahead, he paused to think, and as he did so a sudden gush of water pushed him off his feet and he was nudged towards the side of the road where water ran much deeper. He started floating. Although swimming came naturally to him and he managed to control himself, he realized he had lost his grip on the ground. The water was rising in this part. He glanced around and swam towards the highest object in view, which turned out to be a vegetable vendor's cart, floating itself, but fastened to a shop's gate by a metallic chain. Shahzaada was puzzled to see so much water around, he glanced towards the highway. There was a broad open nullah just before the road met the highway. Shahzaada could see that the nullah was flooded with water gushing with great speed. It looked like a menacing monster gobbling up things that came floating up near it. Shahzaada could see bicycles, wooden carts loaded with vegetables, footwear, garbage, papers, and other things strewn around, being picked up by the flow of the water and disappearing into the deep nullah in seconds. Shahzaada took his eyes off the ghastly sight and glanced further towards the junction, searching for Gattu. The cart on which he stood was wavering in the water and it was difficult for him to focus. Gathering all his concentration he looked again and could make out Gattu's form across the nullah near the highway junction. He seemed half-drowned in the water himself as he tried to help people find their way along with some policeman.

Gattu had reached his traffic duty spot in the morning. He knew that since it was raining the traffic would be slow and that Prakash would need help. He had started helping the policemen around ten in the morning and by late afternoon, he was wading through waist-deep water to go from one point to another. He was scared to see the rising water levels on the road. He had not seen such flooding in his life.

The traffic was coming to a halt; many vehicle's engines were dying down in the water adding to the congestion. The lucky ones, who were able to drive through, were creating more panic in a rush to reach home safely. The heavens were beating the city from all corners. The skies poured buckets and the sea joined in, fuming in fury with high tides. Nature was displaying its might to mortals as if it had an equation to settle.

Prakash told Gattu that a warning had been issued by the government and hence everyone was trying to get home early. Things were expected to get worse. Gattu didn't understand much of the warning. He did not know the security a house brought to a man. He did not know the warmth people felt to be nestled in the confines of a home with their dear ones. He did not know the comfort of lying on a sofa bought with one's own hard-earned money, sipping hot tea, in warm clothes, while the elements wreaked havoc outside. For him, the bench in Munna Bhai's tea stall was the sofa in the afternoon and bed by the night. For him, the awning of the tea stall was his shelter during the rains and Shahzaada, his family, whom he snuggled up to when the weather played truant. For him, it was like any other monsoon day, except that he understood that it was raining much heavier than he had ever seen before.

He stood amidst the rain, drenched, even though wearing a raincoat too large for his size, given by Prakash. His worry for something ominous happening emanated from the worried faces of Prakash and the other policemen who were caught between duty and personal safety. Atmaram had already disappeared as expected but Prakash and JP held the fort. Both were trying to reach their families over mobile phones but the networks seemed jammed. People were ramming into each other's vehicles in a hurry to escape to a haven. The number of people walking on the road was swarming by the hour. People got off the stranded buses, taxis, and autos and preferred to start wading in the water holding each other's hands to keep themselves steady. The water levels around kept rising and the current kept getting stronger. Gattu was overwhelmed with the sight.

Glancing around he saw a huge pile of vehicles near the nullah. He informed Prakash about his intention to go and try to clear the traffic near that side. Whistling hard to get his way cleared, he waded through the water towards the nullah, enjoying the adventure in a way. He felt the current getting stronger as he neared the vehicles stuck on the bridge over the nullah. The wide-open drain was overflowing and it was difficult to say whether it was swallowing the nearby water or vomiting it on the street from its belly. Bottles, cans, vegetables, and other trash came hurtling towards him on their way to be finally sucked into the nullah. Few objects hit Gattu causing him to wince, others he was able to duck. Once or twice he staggered to maintain balance. He no longer seemed amused. From the distance, he heard a familiar shout. Shahzaada! He focused hard in the distance and could see him perched on top of a wooden cart which was part floating. Shahzaada had seen him too and was barking and shaking his tail furiously. Gattu knew from his bark that Shahzaada was not comfortable. Gattu was suddenly worried about him. He started moving quickly towards Shahzaada.

As he moved ahead, Gattu noticed a crowd gathered around the side of the nullah near the railing of the bridge. He inquired about the matter from a man nearby. "A car is stuck, its engine is dead, flooded by water, and someone is stranded inside", the man shouted. Gattu managed to tear his way through the melee towards the area in question, blowing his traffic police whistle when people didn't give way. The nullah crossed the road at almost right angles. Gattu realized that the overflowing water from the nullah had engulfed the entire bridge and was rushing like mad from one side to the other which was a bit downhill. People were stranded on each side of the bridge unable to wade through the rushing water, which was more menacing towards the centre of the bridge. Gattu, being short in stature, almost felt the water reach to his chest as he tried to get closer. He realised it was difficult to proceed this way so he retraced his steps back to a safer place and leapt up a stranded scooter to get a better view of the stuck car.

He could see Shahzaada on the other side of the bridge a bit far away, still atop the cart, and whining slowly. "I will be there soon my boy, just hang on", he shouted to Shahzaada, but the lashing rain and the noise created by the sea of people drowned his voice. Gattu looked around for something to cling on to be able to cross the bridge. The small bridge which would otherwise just take mere forty or fifty steps to cross had now turned into the most treacherous patch for the people on that route. The nullah beneath looked almost like a river, small but mighty in flow. He saw that a few people were gathered clinging around a tree at the other side of the bridge pointing to a small red car stuck in the middle of the bridge. The current was pushing the car sideways, nudging it slowly towards the half-broken cemented railing of the bridge. Most of the people were pointing inside the car.

Gattu raised his heels to get a better view but couldn't make anything out. Towards the uphill side of the bridge, a few people had tied a rope to the tree and had formed a human chain to try and help people stranded on the other side to cross it. Gattu jumped down from the scooter and looked around. He got hold of a length of thin hose pipe from a nearby shop and braved the water again to cross over to the other side to get to Shahzaada. He managed to reach his end of the bridge thanks to the pushing and shoving of others wanting to go in that direction, to utilize the human chain to cross over. As soon as he reached the starting of the bridge, he found himself in the hands of the human chain, which like part of a big moving machinery, started handing him over from arm to arm. As he was being tossed and forwarded closer to his destination, he glanced on the other side of the bridge where the car was battling with the rushing water. The car had started flooding and he could see someone inside on the driver's seat. The loud gush of water and clamour of people around drowned the car driver's voice. Some of the people tried to throw wood and other floating things towards the car to stop it from moving further. He saw a couple of brave people dive towards the car and pull it from behind to steer it clear from the dangerous end having the broken concrete railing. However, the water current proved their efforts futile. Suddenly a gush of water hit the car and it was pushed to the side of the bridge where a huge gap lay open courtesy of the ill maintenance of the local authorities. The car with the dead engine swivelled as the water pushed it from behind. It suddenly rotated to align with the flow of water which forced its front to move off the road, go through the wide gap in the bridge railing and protrude out of the side of the bridge.

Gattu was appalled. The car was now precariously perched on the edge, with the water still thrusting it from behind. A few hands in the human chain stopped to have a look into the matter. It was then that Gattu could see clearly a lady banging the glasses of her car's windows. Gattu went numb, he knew her. He had helped her many times on the crossing holding up the other sides' traffic to let her pass, just to see her smile, which he loved. He remembered the last time he had encountered her with the car's windows rolled down, and he had greeted her stylishly with a "Hello madam".

The human chain had paused, as the car scenario was turning ugly. The hands held him but didn't move forward. Voices could be heard saying, "Why doesn't she just jump out of the car?". Some others said, "Her car is locked due to water corrupting the central locking". Everyone around gaped in horror as the car swivelled and tilted further down into the nullah, with each thrust of the water. The lady continued banging the windows. Then suddenly the hands in the human chain started working again as if the tragedy unfolding in its front was immaterial. In the next few minutes, Gattu managed to reach the other side. He glanced for Shahzaada. Shahzaada had jumped onto a concrete tabletop of a shop and was wriggling his coat dry. "Brave boy", Gattu thought, "He can take care of himself now that he's on sturdier ground". Gattu knew he had to help that lady. He crossed the road from a point the water seemed low and tried getting near the bridge's dangerous side, where the car was struck. Before crossing the road, Gattu accosted one of his friends from the shanties and told him to summon Prakash.

Now getting closer to where the car lay, he constantly kept to the footpath, holding to the shutters of the shops or any other fixtures to be found around for balance. Nearing the bridge, he climbed over a shop through the side pole to get a better view of the car. The car was now tilting badly into the nullah, its front wheels jutted out and were dangling in the air. He knew for certain now that the doors were jammed. "Break the window, break it with something", Gattu shouted, but nobody heard him. However, he realized many folks who had swum to the rear of the car, themselves tied to ropes that others held, were already searching for some objects sturdy enough to break the glass. Some could be heard fearing that hitting the rear windshield, might disbalance the car further, pushing it completely into the nullah, thus endangering the lady's life further. Some were trying to throw ropes around the car, but the raging water made a mockery of the ropes tossing it around on its whim.

Gattu climbed down again and waded through the water to get nearer to the action. "I know her, I know her", he shouted till few people gave him attention. A sturdy young man held his arm and helped him reach nearer. "The water is deep inside the nullah. It's dangerous to go too close to the car. The situation is tricky. If we hit the car with something to break the windshield the impact might push it into the nullah", he heard few men who were gripping a rope providing support to others who surrounded the car, discuss. "We need a crane", someone commented. "Uncle are you joking, where would you get a crane in this weather?". "Do you have the time?", someone else asked, "The car is starting to tilt downwards now", another joined in. "The only way is to tie some ropes to the car and try to pull it back. Few of us will have to swim towards the car. If we can get at least a few ropes tied to the rear, it could work".

Gattu liked this suggestion, however, such a long and sturdy rope was a difficult thing to ask for in a flooded area with waist-deep water and things floating around freely. There were many hardware shops around the bridge but all had shut shop early due to the incessant rains. Everyone looked around frantically. Gattu saw a small truck stranded in the water on the other side of the road. He darted across the water holding the sturdy pipe in his hand for support. He climbed up the back of the truck and looked in the boxes lying around. After some fumbling, he found a thick long rope and cried aloud to the young man on the other side, "I have it, I have it here".

The young man nodded and Gattu threw the rope towards the young man. The rope flew in the air a while, dropped into the water, and floated fast right in the direction of the young man. The young man and an accomplice went towards the back of the car; braving the water and holding on to another rope held by a mass of people standing towards the safer side. They tied the ends of the rope to the rear end of the car and passed the other end to the crowd. People started heaving in on the rope. However, it seemed easier said than done in that gushing water. After a gruelling ten minutes of incessant pulling, the crowd gave up. Some of the people left to attend to their safety and some stopped to re-strategize.

Gattu, who was now part of the rescue team, was getting impatient. He could see the lady inside the car trying to hit the glass with small things she could lay her hands on. She was highly scared. Gattu was wondering what to do next when he saw Prakash arrive at the scene. His SOS seemed to have worked. Gattu ran up to him; tearing through the water and explained the situation to him. Prakash joined the team in pulling the rope but soon understood that the rope needed to be tied to the front and back at several places on the car for the pulling to be able to be any effective. The car was stuck firmly; its base touching on the ground, so pulling it just from behind would not help. He thought of summoning help from the police team to arrange for some heavy vehicle to pull this through but knew it was rather impossible to arrange something and get it on the scene in time, considering the situation in the city. The cell phone networks had long back got congested so he called up a few policemen on the wireless. He summoned a couple of his colleagues at the traffic signal he was posted on, to come to his aid. He also spoke to a few other senior police officials to see if he could get any additional help, but as expected everyone was busy in their own set of crisis management, greater tragedies were unfolding elsewhere. The nearest police van to respond was itself stranded in a flooded area nearby.

While he waited for some other policemen to join him, Prakash carefully steered near the rear of the car, balancing himself in the waist-deep, gushing water to check how to realign the knots of the ropes. Soon JP arrived and he had another rope in his hand. The downpour had increased and they had to shout on top of their voices to communicate. Prakash called to JP, "We need the other rope tied to the front or the center of the car else we will not be able to pull effectively". "But how's that possible, the car is perched precariously, the front is almost halfway hanging in the air, on top of the nullah"; JP shouted back.

Prakash nodded to JP, "Let me try". He left the rope he was clinging to and went around the car to the railing of the nullah. Prakash tried opening the doors of the car but as expected they were jammed. By this time Gattu had braved the waters and managed to reach the end of the rope tied to the car. He could feel the water thrusting against his chest. He hung on to the rope tightly to maintain his balance. Prakash was clinging to the cemented railing of the bridge. He had one end of the other rope that JP had bought. He tried to fling it across the car trying to cover it from the center. But he knew soon that it was a difficult task, the wind, rain, and flowing water tossed the rope like a feather, making it impossible to land in the correct places. JP cried to Prakash. "It's useless, let's try to break the window, we have to take the chance".

Prakash realized JP was right, there was no use taking the rope strategy further. They had to take calculated risks. Gattu who had heard the conversation, reasoned with Prakash, "Throwing anything heavy from behind to break the rear windshield might push the car further down, it might even fall in the nullah". But by the time he and Prakash could think, they saw JP rushing to the rear side, a metal fire extinguisher in his hands. Before Prakash could say stop, JP had already flung the cylinder with force towards the rear windshield of the car. The impact partially damaged the glass, making a small hole towards the bottom. That provided a new vent for the water to seep into the car. The fire extinguisher went off as well, spreading foam on the entire rear windshield and the water around. And then it disappeared in the nullah after emptying its contents. The confusion seemed to have increased. The lady, who was hurt a bit by the sudden impact, now started crying vehemently because of the water trickling in.

"JP what did you do?", Prakash cried. He was now nervous as the lady had started moving and thumping wildly from within the car and the car was swinging due to the movement. She was not realizing but it was inching slowly towards the depths of the nullah. "Madam", Prakash shouted, "Please stay calm and don't move too much". The lady either didn't hear it or was too panicked. The situation was getting worse. Gattu made a sudden decision, "I'm going in, I'm lighter in weight, I can try to do something". Before Prakash could ask him why or how Gattu thrust the rope's end that he held, in Prakash's hands and darted towards the bridge's railing. Prakash saw Gattu reach the railing and try to climb it. "JP give me the other rope", he commanded. Prakash threw the free rope towards Gattu, "Here, take this". Gattu obliged and taking the rope in the hand climbed up the railing, crouching once on top of it. Gattu realized that it was not a very easy situation to be in. The railing was slippery, it even seemed weak to him, and it wavered as water flew past the openings below. "Gattu, hold on to the rope tightly. You are too small, it's dangerous, you should not be up there". Before Prakash could say anything else Gattu started moving towards the car slowly, occasionally standing completely, occasionally crouching, to maintain balance. Prakash clung to the rope tightly fearing Gattu might slip and fall and hit the nullah. JP was murmuring, "What a fool, what's he doing?". Prakash shouted back, "I am not sure what he has in mind, but we have to play by this now. Pulling out is risky, just ensure you are around". Gattu reached the side of the car from where the railing was broken. He could see that the car's front wheels were jetting out into the nullah, fighting to stay against the water dropping below into the nullah in rage. Suddenly Prakash's heart leapt as he saw Gattu jump onto the car, balancing himself on the top of the car.

Prakash moved the rope and tightened his grip. Gattu held onto the rope for dear life, all his balance depending on it. The car swivelled. The lady inside had her mouth agape.

"Gattu, stay towards the rear, balance it out", Prakash shouted. Gattu understood the instruction. Clinging tightly to the rope, he moved towards the rear of the car and balanced himself sitting down, spreading his legs on top of the rear windshield. The car seemed better balanced now. Gattu hit the rear windshield with his leg repeatedly to no avail. By that time JP had arranged a hammer from somewhere, he made a loop around the hammer and slid it along the rope. "Use this Gattu", he shouted. Gattu reached out to the hammer which slowly slid towards him on the rope. "Target the front window instead", Prakash shouted, "And hit the edge towards the base". Gattu had to cautiously balance himself as he had slipped a few times trying to lift himself. His legs hurt. He decided to move slowly towards the front still sitting on the top of the car, legs dangling on the sides. He hit the windows as soon as his hands could reach the window. One blow and the next one and the glass finally shattered. The crowd cheered. Gattu retracted some of the rope he was using and handed over his end to the lady telling her to hold on to it.

What Prakash saw next was something he would never forget for the rest of his life. A tilted red car ready to nose dive into the nullah at one bad move, Gattu balancing himself with a rope on top of the car and the lady trying to pull herself out of the window. People around gaped in horror as the car swung back and forth. "Gattu get out of there, she has the rope now", Prakash commanded. But Gattu seemed determined to get the job done. The lady was creeping out of the car slowly, the rope in one hand. Suddenly as Gattu shifted his weight on top of the car for her to emerge he slid towards the bonnet. The car moved wildly due to the impact. The lady panicked and rushed out of the window. The sudden jerks, as she shoved her way out, pushed the car further and it skidded wildly towards the nullah, only to be stopped by the rear wheels getting stuck in the bottom of the bridge. The lady managed to jump to the side railing while this happened but as she did that, she pushed the car back with her feet. Gattu who was clinging to the rope and the bonnet of the car was thrown into the nullah due to the sudden jerk, his head hitting the cemented side on his way down. Prakash and others shuddered. Prakash tugged on the rope. It was free!

The people around rushed to the lady's side making a human chain to assist each other. Prakash gave the rope to JP and rushed towards the end of the bridge, without support, tripping, falling, floating in between, and crying aloud "Gattu, Gattu!". He reached the sidewall, clung to it with both hands, and looked below. Gattu was nowhere to be seen. Prakash kept on crying out his name. He could see a streak of blood gushing towards the area where the nullah took full force and met the main drain, swollen up like a gushing river today. Prakash's eyes wandered desperately for a clue of Gattu. The stream of blood soon became more prominent and thicker and suddenly, it mixed into the foaming waters and disappeared. A while later Prakash saw Gattu's policemen's cap which he wore on duty, popping out of the water towards the main drain, floating aimlessly as the water played with it.

Prakash shouted to JP to get some help, get some divers, but in his heart, he knew the futility of his demand. Prakash looked at the cap tirelessly, tears streaming down his eyes, as the other people around helped the woman to safety. The cap wobbled up and down for a further few minutes, and then a sudden gush of water made it flow to the area where the blood streak had disappeared. It wobbled slowly there for some time and then drowned, lost forever. Prakash moved back slowly; head hung in distress.

A mournful howl came from afar. Prakash looked up and saw a sturdily built dog standing atop a concrete table top, mouth pointed towards the sky, wailing mournfully!

2

LEOPARD IN POWAI

Keshav stealthily opened the door to his house. He was coming late from work and did not want to disturb his father's sleep. Keshav was a senior underwriter with a multinational insurance company. His job constantly required him to work late hours. By the time he usually reached home, his father would already be asleep. Today, however, as he entered the house, he found the lights glowing in the bedroom. He walked up to the entrance of the room and saw his father up in bed, flipping the pages of a daily newspaper. "Dad, is everything okay? I hope you are feeling well?" he enquired, genuinely concerned. His father merely nodded back and continued gazing at the newspaper.

For more than a year since Keshav's mother's death, his father had renounced himself from the outside world. He was no longer interested in anything. His outlook towards life had changed completely. He chose to remain solitary most of the time. Keshav and he rarely talked. They just sat together to eat their breakfast and occasionally dinner, when Keshav could manage to get home on time. Apart from this, he kept himself confined to his room either sitting on his chair or lying on the bed, brooding about things that Keshav had no idea of. Doctors had told Keshav that his father was suffering from severe clinical depression. Keshav had tried many avenues to bring his father out of this state but had failed each time.

It was therefore rather surprising for Keshav to see his father brooding over the newspaper today, so late at night. Realizing his son's curious glances upon him; Keshav's father soon folded the paper, lied down, and went to sleep. Keshav went to his bedside and switched off the light, carrying the newspaper with him. Once in his room, he looked at the front page of the newspaper, his eyes searching for the news that had caught his father's attention. The search wasn't very difficult. On the cover page was a photograph of a leopard caught in a cage. The adjacent headline screamed, "Leopard kills man in Mumbai". Alongside another small article read: "Ecologists doubt city builders' plans". Keshav smiled. His father was a retired professor. He had taught environmental science in the prestigious Institute of Technological Innovations in Powai and his favourite subject was Ecology.

The next morning when Keshav woke up and crossed his father's room, he found him awake, sitting by the window, newspaper in his hand. He held the newspaper close to his face straining to read the words. Keshav moved on to the kitchen, made himself some coffee, and then went to sit beside his father. "What's up dad?" he inquired. His father shook his head slightly still focusing on the newspaper. Keshav got up and went to the table in the far corner of the room. He brought out an old pair of spectacles from the drawer and gave them to his father. "Here, you always keep them in the drawer and forget about them. What's so interesting in the newspaper?", he asked. "There's a leopard in Powai", his father murmured, almost to himself. "It happened some seven years ago when we lived by the lakeside that a man-eater was spotted in our area. Now another one seems to have entered our locality", he continued. Keshav listened to his father intently, not for the information he was imparting but for the fact that after a long time a meaningful conversation was building between them.

"Yes, I heard somewhere", Keshav responded. "For the past one week, there have been various incidents in different areas in the city adjoining the forest sanctuary. And now it's Powai". Keshav sipped his coffee. "When was the first one spotted?" his father inquired. "About six days earlier. A man had gone for his early morning walk near the forest area when the leopard struck", Keshav replied. "Is that coffee?" his father asked suddenly inhaling the aroma. Keshav nodded, smiling. "Half a cup for me!" the old man ordered, burying himself in the newspaper again.

Keshav had been born and brought up in Mumbai and yet the bustling cosmopolitan's wonders had never ceased to amaze him. As he travelled from his office to home in the public bus, he was amazed at the myriad terrain that the city offered. Mountains, lakes, beaches, creeks, and forests, all formed a part of the vibrant city.

Amongst one such wonder was the forest reserve in the city's suburbs. The expansive forest area was home to a vast variety of flora and fauna. Once distant from the main city, it had now been engulfed by the unsatiated needs of human habitation thus putting pressure on its periphery. And hence human-animal conflicts had increased. The one animal most infamous for such conflict was the leopard. Every now and then a leopard would stray out of the forest area and attack humans or their domesticated animals. Conservationists would track this to the unavailability of sufficient prey within the forest. The people would blame improper boundaries at the reserve and government apathy. The forest department would come up with a fresh reason each season. This time around they turned their guns towards the builders whom they accused of building houses too close to the reserve area. The poor slum dweller at the periphery of the reserve suffered the most. Their poultry, pet animals, and open-door huts were invitation enough for a straying big cat looking for easy prey.

A day later Keshav was puzzled not to find his father in his room when he returned from work. Worried, he searched the kitchen and the toilet and, in the end, found him on the balcony. He stood standing, gazing at the vast green expanse of mountains that lay ahead. "Dad, what are you doing here?" he asked. The old man did not respond but kept staring at the darkness ahead. They remained silent for a while. Then the old man spoke slowly. "Keshav, isn't it a great feeling to know that there is a big powerful animal out there, very close to us, watching our every move". He smiled slightly. "Dad the newspapers are crying hoarse about the increasing attacks, people are afraid to step out of their houses, the number of people dying has increased and you say it's a great feeling?", Keshav scoffed, unbuttoning his sweat-drenched, dusty shirt. His father gave a small laugh, "At least we are still afraid of something! Besides all this has nothing to do with the poor creature. It's our problem that we decided to dwell so near to its home. There's no cruelty or wrong doing on his part. It's mismanagement and greed on ours! Aren't we slicing each other's throats every day in the guise of competition? Why people even kill each other over petty matter these days. That poor animal is only attacking to feed, to keep itself alive". By now Keshav was smiling wryly. He was enjoying this discussion. It was after months he had such a long conversation with his father. Something had stirred within the old man and he seemed to be his former self today. Keshav felt delighted.

The next morning as Keshav passed by his father's room, he saw his father meditating. A sudden happiness surged through Keshav. He had always seen his father do yoga in the morning without fail till he went into depression. It was heartening for him to see the old man picking up a few things from the past. After he had finished, Keshav brought his father a cup of warm milk as he flipped through the newspaper to grab what he wanted. "Dad, I see the ecologist in you has arisen", he smiled. The old man nodded in agreement. "The nature-man balance is a very interesting topic, son. Few people take it seriously but it's vital to understand and address it in today's fast-changing world". Keshav's father started pacing the room as if addressing a class. Keshav listened intently like the most obedient student in the world. Their discussion dwelt upon related topics like human habitat around the forest, the slum dwellers, and their problems. The retired professor conveyed to his son about what could be done versus what was being done by the authorities. "Dad, how are you so aware of such recent happenings? The newspaper doesn't cover these details I know for sure", Keshav enquired a bit puzzled. "Well, I have been watching a bit of television in the day when you are away. So many local channels are covering the news, you know", his father stated unreservedly. Keshav's heart leapt with joy.

A few days later, a couple of former students came to visit the retired professor. It was Teacher's Day and they wanted to greet him. Keshav was happily surprised by finding his father willing to meet the visitors. The professor had hardly met a handful of people, mostly well-wishers from the neighbourhood, in the last six months. The old man recognized each of his students and chatted and laughed with them sharing the old memories. After they left, the old man walked into Keshav's room. "They presented me something", he held out a book towards Keshav. It was Jim Corbett's 'The man-eating leopard of Rudraprayag' and on the cover page was a growling picture of a magnificent leopard.

That night after dinner Keshav asked, "Have you ever seen a leopard dad, I mean in the wild?". "No son, only once or twice in the zoo. They are swift creatures, very hard to track down in the wild. But I have seen a Tiger up close in the Corbett National Park and I can tell you it's an enthralling experience. When you go to such a place and have such magnificent experiences, you realize that it's your responsibility to protect and nurture all the beauty that is there in this world. It's our duty if we think of ourselves as the most evolved species on the earth". The old man went about detailing his experiences in the jungle to the son who lapped up every minute of the discussion.

Keshav felt his father's voice breaking on his ears. "Keshav, get up, it's important", Keshav woke up startled. "What happened dad, everything all right?" he inquired. He found his father dressed up in his best trouser and shirt. "A leopard has been caught near the lake. They are going to take him away soon. Come let's have a look before they do so". Keshav darted to the washroom in a dizzy, still absorbing what he heard.

That night when they were together again on the balcony, Keshav asked softly, "Dad what would they do to him?". "Release him deep inside the jungle most probably; it wasn't a man-eater after all". "And what if it returns?". "We can only hope it doesn't", the old man smiled.

Slowly, as the monsoon died in the city, the stray visits of the leopards lessened. The newspapers found other happenings to flash on their cover pages. People shifted their attention to the festive season at hand. The slum dwellers earlier scared away by the leopard attacks, once again returned to occupy places at the reserve's periphery. Everything turned normal.

Keshav entered his house stealthily, not wanting to disturb his father's sleep. He found him awake, sitting in front of the television, well shaved and neatly dressed in his kurta pyjama, picking on a bowl of fruit salad in his hand. "What's up dad? Now what? Crocodile trouble in Powai?", Keshav laughed. "No son, guess what, it's historic! India won a gold at the Olympics", the old man beamed brightly.

3

A Phone Call

Moshi Moshi – is a Japanese phrase for "hello" while starting a conversation on the phone. It sounds almost like Mushi Mushi when spoken.

The Yurikamome gained speed, finally finding a straight undulated stretch after a moderate climb to reach the entrance to the magnificent Rainbow bridge in Tokyo. It was ten past midnight and the train was quite packed. Keigo was lucky enough to find a seat for himself when he boarded the train from Ariake. He was returning from work; his day had been a maze of confusion. His manager was out of the country, visiting India on a business trip and he had been put in charge. Keigo was a part of a large Japanese electronics corporation and having worked with them for over five years now, he knew the game. He was doing a real good job of managing things while his manager was away. However, today had been different. One of his clients, an old grumpy man, a higher-up with one of the government banks, had suddenly shown up in the office and started complaining about the specifications of a consignment of printers he had been delivered from Keigo's organization. He was pointing to the absence of a new feature in the printers that Keigo's manager had allegedly promised him. He demanded to get the order updated immediately and Keigo had no clue of how to do it without knowing the details. He had tried contacting his manager a couple of times during the day on his mobile phone but always found him unreachable. He had then escalated the matter to his senior management who came rushing to his help. They pacified the client and ensured him a fast resolution. They also assured Keigo that they would track down his manager to get the details on what had to be done.

Now, sitting in the Yurikamome gently chugging towards his house in Hinode, western Tokyo, he could feel his lower back aching due to the innumerous time he bowed in front of the client to tender his apology for not meeting their expectations. He felt his phone vibrate in his coat's pocket. "Moshi, Moshi", he spoke, picking up the phone. It was one of the management seniors who had promised to get back to him after tracking Keigo's supervisor. "Hai, Arighato gosaimas!", Keigo said disconnecting the call after listening briefly to the other side. He had been provided a local cell phone number in India which his manager was carrying, and had been suggested to contact him. Keigo glanced out of the window of the moving train, heaving a sigh of relief. "Finally, I would be able to close this issue after a call with Takeishi-san", he thought. The city lights glowed in the distance reflecting in the waters of the Tokyo bay, on which the towering suspension bridge stretched. Keigo looked at his phone and thought for a while. His station was approaching. He decided that he would give a call to Takeishi-san once he got off the train. He started gazing absent-mindedly at the vehicles zipping by the train from both sides on the roads that ran parallel to the train tracks.

Aslam gobbled down his keema pav greedily. It took him hardly three minutes to wipe his plate clean. His hunger still unsatiated, he ordered a repeat and glanced at his mobile screen to check on the time. It was still a good thirty minutes before nine. He flipped the phone in his palms, the latest Nokia model, smaller in size, no protruding antenna, a novelty for sure, and a great soft keypad, a deviation from the hard plastic or metal ones found in the other models. He was fascinated with the phone especially when it glowed beaming different coloured lights while ringing.

The small restaurant he was sitting in was about to close and the last orders for the day were being served. The harried waiter who had taken Aslam's order a while back returned, manipulating a tray at least ten times bigger than his palm, on which he carried the food. He came gliding amongst the maze of tables so efficiently that Aslam was forced to strain his neck downwards towards the waiter's feet to check whether he was wearing skates. Aslam guffawed upon confirming the obvious, as the waiter reached his table and banged the plate containing another helping of keema pav on his table. The impact made the lemon slice that came as an accompaniment to the dish, jump from the plate and fall into Aslam's lap. Before Aslam could absorb what had happened, the waiter had already glided to another table serving the next order.

Aslam sighed, putting the lemon slice back onto his plate and helping himself to the food in front of him. The poor waiter must be tired by now, he thought. After all, it was almost the end of the day for most while he was still awake and working.

Aslam attacked his second serving of keema pav and was done in another four minutes. Once finished he felt his stomach full but missing something. He realized that he needed something to douse the fire in his belly that the spicy food had flared. He felt the ulcers in his stomach yell at him in anger for feasting on such hot food. He could hear his wife's shrill voice in his ears, yelling, "Remember what the doctor advised? No spicy food!". "Balls!", he swore under his breath! He knew that doctor Pandey whom he was consulting for his stomach-related issues, was himself found more on the nearby fast food stall than in his dingy clinic. "Try khichdi yourself, twice, as the doctors say B-D, and remember to add lemon to make it tastier", he felt compelled to suggest Pandey each time he visited him and heard his rant about eating simple food. But he had to curtail his frustration because of his wife who always accompanied him. Not that he cared for her getting mad at him for giving it back to Pandey, but more because he never got a chance to speak. Pandey directed all his questions to Mumtaz, his wife as if she was the patient, and Mumtaz reciprocated doubly well as if she was herself bringing up the ulcers he housed in his stomach. He sometimes doubted what the purpose of the visit was, his health or the coochie-cooing between Pandey and Mumtaz.

The burning sensation in his stomach interfered with his thoughts. He pulled out the long, laminated menu card from beneath a small porcelain vase kept at the centre of the table. The vase contained a single artificial rose with a stem and leaves. The leaves were more black than green and the flower petals were torn at the edges. Aslam pulled out the rose from the vase while going through the items on the menu card to shortlist his next order. He absent-mindedly sniffed the artificial rose and coughed aloud as he did so. It smelled foul and dusty. He quickly put it back and glanced around to see if someone had noted his act of foolishness. Once he was assured that it was not the case, he snapped his fingers to get the attention of the waiter who had taken his previous order. The waiter, ever attentive to such gestures, glanced in his direction and came gliding through the tables to him. Aslam glanced at the waiter's feet again, "Still no skates, how does he do it"; he sighed. "A Lemon Soda", he ordered. "Last orders done, already told you before", the waiter replied crisply. Aslam was caught off guard and before he could mouth any of his favourite expletives, the waiter was gone. Aslam was enraged. He banged the table and whistled in the direction of the waiter. The waiter just waved his hands from a distance as if telling him to hold. The rejection at the hands of the waiter and the fire in his belly elevated his anger. He walked over to the waiter, who had just started to clean up an empty table. Confronting him, Aslam shouted, "You know who I am? See this?". He pulled up his shirt and pointed towards his belly to make the waiter see the butt of the revolver he carried. "Will stick this into you if you don't bring me my order". The waiter simply saw the man in front of him pointing to his belly. He smirked, "Stick what?". His quirky smile made Aslam glance down. "Damn", he said realizing that the butt of his 0.25 gun was not to be seen on his hairy dark belly. He realized that it had slid into his underwear completely and he fumbled to pull it back. The waiter, grinning now at the proceedings, conceded. "I get it. You really need a lemon soda. I will get it". He rushed off.

Back on his table, Aslam adjusted his gun, pulling the butt out so that it did not tangle with the bulge between the crotch. He wondered why his attempts at any kind of heroism always lead to embarrassment. He glanced at the mobile phone in his hand. It was few minutes past nine. "The phone is expected anytime now"; he thought. He started sipping the soda that the waiter placed on his table, staring at the screen of his phone blankly.

Aslam was a jack of many trades. Living in the southern part of Mumbai, he owned a small shop selling cheap mobile phones and accessories. The shop was operated mostly by his younger brother with Aslam overlooking the operations from a distance. Aslam also dabbled in real estate, albeit at a macro level. He played a middle man on a commission basis to fix up deals for people looking to buy or rent a dwelling in or around the chawl where he lived. His USP, unlike the other estate agents around, lay in the fact that he carried a gun in his pocket that he occasionally flashed to seal the deal in his favour. This gun was a sign of his association with the local mafia gangs that dotted that part of the city.

The shop and the estate brokerage job gave him enough money to run his house but his association with the Chajju master gang was more for power than for any monetary gains. Aslam was, until some time ago, primarily assigned to facilitating the transfer of smuggled material from one person to another. He was a mere cog in a giant machinery that neither knew what the machine was doing nor where it belonged in the larger picture. Tired of this, he had pleaded to his ustad, his senior and mentor Jadhav, to get him meatier work. He had assured Jadhav of his risk-taking abilities and had implored him to talk to the others in the chain to get him something that would make him feel that he was indeed part of a crime gang. Jadhav saw the keenness in Aslam and helped him upgrade his profile by making him a conduit for the transfer of weapons like pistols, guns, or rifles. This had excited Aslam as in many cases he got to meet some local notorious charge sheeters and criminals personally while delivering them weapons for their next strike. It was on one such assignment that he had met Kripal. He didn't know him at first, neither was Kripal's name of any value in his circle. Until a few days earlier when the local TV channels beamed the CCTV footage of a jewellery store in Bhendi Bazaar, where Kripal was seen, looting jewellery, and killing one of the shopkeepers in the melee that ensued. Something inside Aslam had stirred on watching that clip. The gun used in the crime was the one he had delivered to Kripal. Aslam had felt a certain sense of achievement that day. He was confused about whether it was good to feel the way he felt, elated, but he soon appeased himself that if he had to get any deeper into the gang, this feeling was just fine to nurture. Somewhere in his heart he even wanted to be at the scene of the crime, yielding the pistol himself.

It was this thought that spurred Aslam to meet Jadhav again and talk about his ambitions. Jadhav had given him a patient hearing but had dismissed his plea initially, terming it a mere rush of blood. However, on Aslam's consistent insistence he put in a word to his higher-ups. After that Aslam was assigned to assist on a kidnapping in which he fared handsomely. That was followed by a couple of heists where he came up trumps as well. Impressed with the rookie's performance Aslam was then assigned a more challenging task and one that he had eventually dreamt of. Murder!

Aslam had been given a brief about the plan by Jadhav who was supposed to be his partner in crime on the case. A mole had been detected within their gang and had to be eliminated. His name was not confirmed and the brief mentioned that it would be declared at the last moment to keep the operation a secret. There was just a hint that it might be someone they already knew.

Aslam had put in all his intellect to analyse who it could be. He suspected Jagan, the part-time tea stall owner who indulged in the activities for the gang in parallel, to be the culprit. He had seen him hobnobbing with some plainclothes policemen a few times. He had also considered Akram Ustad and Mushtaq, popularly known as Mushi. However, his final assessment absolved them based on the fidelity they had always shown to the group since the last many years. Jagan was his contender for the hit.

The brief had said that the name would be disclosed over a call late at night on the day of the operation. Aslam's cell phone number had been forwarded to the higher-ups and Jadhav had mentioned that the call was expected to be via an international number as the decision will be taken at the round table meeting of the bosses who were currently sheltered in China.

Keigo got off the train at Hinode station which was a quick walk from the apartment he lived in. As he descended the escalator, he fumbled for the piece of paper in his pocket on which he had written down his manager's temporary phone number. Once in his hands, he flipped open his mobile phone and tapped the digits on the keyboard. He touched the prepaid Suica card to exit the station gates as he listened to the beeps of the network trying to connect. He stopped suddenly as the beeps gave way to a ring. A phone rang 4000 miles away in Mumbai.

His hunger well satiated, Aslam stood outside the eatery, checking out a few nubile girls gathered in a group on the street. It was dark and the street was changing its hue. The professional side of the metro was retiring to its home and many nocturnal nefarious activities were now coming into being. The girls outside the restaurant, with whom Aslam was engaging with his deft eye language, were part of one such setup. He didn't mean business at the moment due to the important work at hand, but habit made him pry nonetheless. He tore his eyes off a dusky-looking girl, as the phone rang loudly. He winced as he realized his son had changed the ringtone to a trendy Bollywood song not suitable for his age. He heard the girls giggle in the background on his choice of ringtone but he had no time for anger. He looked at the display, an international call indeed, the moment had arrived! "Hello", he said confidently, picking up the phone.

"Moshi, Moshi", the voice on the other side said. "Mushi? ", questioned Aslam. Aslam's head spun a bit. So Mushi it was. "Are you sure?", he questioned despite having being warned not to ask any question to the caller. The voice on the other end uttered again, "Hai, Moshi Moshi". "Okay got it, its Mushi, right?". The voice on the other end paused and then the call got disconnected.

The cards had been opened. Mushi was the informer in the group, the mole, the traitor that had to be punished. Aslam never thought Mushi could do such a thing. He was so serious at his work. But maybe that's why he did things so efficiently. The decision was not to be deliberated over by him.

He had his orders. He merely had to execute. Aslam glanced at his watch. He knew Mushi would be found with his girlfriend at his second home, away from the clutches of his possessive wife. Aslam sighed, "What a lucky man. He's able to handle two ladies at this age while men half his age were already running towards the hermitage to commit penance for the one big mistake they committed in their life, that of marriage". Aslam grinned at his thought. "But not any longer. Mushi's luck is out now!", Aslam thought as he headed for the kill.

Mushtaq Khan or Mushi, as he was more popularly known, was a full-time associate of the Chajju Master gang. He ran a small shop dealing in electronics to provide a legal face to his illegal occupation. Most of the inventory in his store incidentally came from the customs department's sale of confiscated goods. Mushi's good rapport with some officials ensured he bagged the cream of such products at throwaway rates even before they reached the bidder's conference.

Mushi was one of the most active members of the Chajju gang in the area Aslam lived in. He maintained a stoic and serious profile, although being involved in many high-profile cases of murders and thefts.

Aslam parked the taxi, a weathered Fiat borrowed from a friend exclusively for this mission, a few blocks before the house where he expected Mushi to be found. It was a small double-storied chawl. Mushi's girlfriend lived on the upper floor, in the second house from the staircase landing. Aslam walked slowly towards the chawl, checking whether he had taken all the necessary precautions. He had put the silencer on his gun and had changed the number plate of the taxi to a fake one. He had put on a black sports cap on his head and plain glasses on his eyes to change his looks. He planned to bring Mushi out of the house on some pretext, lead him to the deserted spot where he had parked the taxi and then do what was expected.

Before Aslam softly knocked on the door with the gang's trademark tapping style, he removed his cap and glasses to ensure Mushi recognized him instantly. Aslam had earlier worked with the gang to deliver Mushi the equipment to execute some of his infamous crimes. So Mushi didn't suspect any foul play when he saw Aslam at his door in the dead of the night. What Mushi was confused about though was the timing of Aslam's visit. He hadn't gotten any intimation from the higher-ups on any new assignments or delivery and was in a rather relaxed mood. "What's it this time?"; he enquired. "You will have to come out with me, can't discuss here, have something to show"; Aslam murmured, his eyes focused in the background where Mushi's lady love could be seen lying cosily on the bed.

"Wait outside, I'll change"; Mushi commanded as he shut the door on Aslam's face.

As Aslam waited outside the house, he started thinking about the girl on Mushi's bed. He recalled her name as Hema, he had met her a couple of times earlier when he had visited Mushi's house to deliver consignments. He remembered how gleefully he had gobbled the sweets which he had been offered by her, when he had asked her for merely a glass of water, on the last such meeting. He recalled how she had smiled notoriously as her hands had brushed past Aslam's legs while setting up the table and how he had almost jumped apologetically.

Now when Mushi's gone, she will need another man to take

care of her, Aslam thought. He could imagine himself at Mushi's funeral, offering his shoulders to Hema for support, after all, who else did she know in the vicinity. He decided he would bring her fruits and food each day after Mushi was gone. Maybe some wine too on special occasions, he grinned to himself. Good that she was asleep and hadn't seen him. Nobody will know what happened. His theatrically inspired dreaming was broken by the sound of the door unlocking. Mushi stepped out, a heavy gun in his hand. Aslam froze, "What do you need this for?", he muttered. "Never step out of the house without this you fool, it's a necessity in our business", Mushi chided playfully. Aslam decided not to question further lest he may cause some suspicion.

Killing Mushi wasn't very difficult for Aslam. He knew he had a barbaric side to him, which made it very easy for him to shoot anyone and not brood about it before or after the crime. What he had found difficult instead was the small talk he had to do with Mushi as he guided him to the parked taxi. "What stuff have you got this time? Strange I don't have any instructions on this".

"Well, there's a taxi parked outside the compound, let's go there". "Oh, the stuff's in the taxi?", Mushi enquired. "Yes"; Aslam said tersely. "Why taxi, why couldn't you have brought Jadhav's car? Is it a big consignment or something?". "Hmm... It's big", Aslam muttered, uncomfortable with the way the conversation was going.

"Who gave it to you, the consignment"; Mushi continued. "I don't know". "What do you mean by that, someone must have passed it on to you to deliver to me, right? Or you generated it yourself?", Mushi teased Aslam. "You seem constipated", Mushi babbled on, not able to elicit a response from Aslam.

"What happened, had too much of your favourite keema pav in dinner?", Mushi guffawed.

By this time, they had reached the taxi. Aslam opened the boot, swiftly took out the revolver that he had kept there, turned, and shot Mushi in his chest three times without batting an eyelid.

"Why did you have to ask so many questions?", was the only thing he muttered.

Aslam was dragging Mushi into the rear seat of the taxi when he saw a familiar figure rushing toward the taxi. He froze. Was he dreaming or did he see Hema walking towards him?

She was still far off and he could only see her silhouette, but he knew it was her. He rushed and shoved Mushi's body completely inside the taxi, closed the rear door, jumped on the driver's seat, and brought the engine to life. He put the vehicle into reverse gear but by that time Hema was already behind the taxi. Aslam looked in the rear mirror, perplexed what to do next. He saw she had a hairbrush in her hand. "Poor girl, she must've been braiding her hair, when she would have realized Mushi was missing", he thought. "Wait, but wasn't she sleeping when I visited Mushi? So why the comb?". He glanced in the side mirror to get a better view. He saw Hema raise the hairbrush in his direction. "Hold on you swine, stop right there!", she shouted. She's threatening me with a comb, or is it…. a…a GUN!", Aslam froze. Hema was a gangster's girlfriend, she would step out with a gun rather than a comb for sure, Aslam cursed himself for being so naïve.

"Whoever you are, I saw what you did", Hema shouted. Aslam pushed the throttle and moved the car back breaking in jerks, wanting to threaten her. "You don't get it, I saw what you did to Mushi, come out and put your hands on your head"; he heard her screaming. "So, you can see them? Go on complete the dialogue, you policewoman", Aslam shouted back failing to check the movie buff in him. This caught Hema off guard. The voice seemed familiar. Aslam knew he couldn't run the taxi over her. So, without thinking too much, he got out of the car and faced Hema. "It's me, Aslam!"

Aslam soon realized that Hema didn't love Mushi after all. She was just living with him to cover up for her expenses that she couldn't meet despite working as a beautician at a nearby salon. When Aslam told her his assignment nonchalantly, Hema too opened up in the same vein. She rolled her eyes and clicked her tongue as she gave Aslam her offer, "I am sure you will be getting some money after this assignment. Fifty percent of that to me, and I have seen nothing", she winked. Aslam was flabbergasted. He should have run her over after all! "No, I wouldn't get so much sweetheart that I could share between the two of us", he retorted sardonically. "I just spared your life a minute ago by not running you over, remember?", he quipped. "Oh my, you wouldn't have done that, I know. I can see you get weak in your knees when you see me", Hema said smirking and getting closer to him. "Behold, the dove that I was eyeing turned out to be a vulture"; Aslam taunted. Hema clapped softly at the theatrics and gazed at Aslam with wide eyes, standing her ground.

Aslam weighed his options, kill her, and clean the slate or deny her anything and let her crib but risk her going to the police. Or give her some money and shut her up, after all with her absconding the prime suspect would be her, in case anybody questioned Mushi's whereabouts.

"Twenty-five grand and no more", he said, "and remember, the police will search for you in case someone files a report". "Fifty is what I agree to. As for the report it's highly unlikely, nobody misses a missing gangster", Hema replied sarcastically. She was smart, much smarter than he imagined. He knew it was a fair deal. "Ok, so you better disappear and remember not to open your mouth ...ever!". "Or...", he continued softening his voice, "if you want to be around, I could … you know….", he faltered for words. "Take care of me?"; Hema said pouting her lips. Aslam felt goose bumps. But suddenly he saw her expression change. "You are not a bad man Aslam, but not a great one either! Don't get me wrong but I have had my share with the likes of Mushi and you. I'll take the money and try starting afresh somewhere else"; Hema looked forlorn as she spoke.

As Aslam drove the taxi towards the graveyard where he had already made provisions for the burial, he pondered whether he had done the right thing by letting Hema go. He was told to keep some money stashed away in the car, in case someone somewhere had to be bribed to get past to safety. He had utilized part of that to give to Hema. He was unsure whether what he had done was out of logic or simply his crush on her. His thoughts were interrupted by the ringing of the phone. It was almost the same international number the earlier call had come from. "Now what? Do they want to check on his burial?", he sighed

"Hello", he picked up the phone.

"It's Kripal", the voice at the other end said. "What, who...", muttered Aslam. "Kripal...uhh..."; the voice at the other end paused, then came back. "The sun shines in the...?". "Night", Aslam replied, completing the answer to the question he had memorized a day before. This was supposed to be the code for the assignment if necessary. "Good"; the voice over the phone replied. "It's Kripal, repeat Kripal", and the line went dead.

Aslam's head spun. He pulled over the taxi to the side and mulled over what he had just heard. "Why did they call me twice? And how could it be both Mushi and Kripal?". Did that mean the day was not over for him yet and he had to commit another murder on the day of his first meaningful association with the gang? He vividly recalled being told it was a single person who was to be murdered. He froze as the thought struck him that the first caller had not asked for the secret question's answer. He consoled himself with the fact that Jadhav had told him that the answer to the code was not always asked. He turned around and looked at Mushi's body in the rear. He knew he had to call up Jadhav to seek clarification.

Jadhav was, expectedly, perplexed, and furious over what was happening. "How can it be both Mushi and Kripal, use your brain, Aslam!". "And where did you get the two calls from? Look at the numbers are they the same?". "No bhai, they are different, although both from China". He could feel Jadhav seething with anger on the other line. "Send me both numbers on SMS and stay tight till I call you back!"

Five minutes later Aslam's ears were being pounded with the choicest of expletives by Jadhav. He was so loud that Aslam who had kept the phone a good half foot away from his ears, was still able to hear him properly. "You uneducated scum, don't you know the difference between a number starting with

+80 and +81, how could they be from the same country. Have you sold your brain to your favourite keema pav vendor?", Jadhav continued. "The second call was from China", Jadhav roared. After a good 5 minutes of shouting at Aslam, who meekly listened to the deluge, Jadhav regained his composure. He realized something was fishy, even if the person calling from the other number was fake why did he still utter Mushi's name? Was there more than met the eye? Was their plan leaked?

"What next Bhai?", checked Aslam feebly, finally managing to speak. "I have confirmed that the real orders were for Kripal. We will figure out about Mushi's case later, but first, we have to knock off Kripal"; Jadhav replied. "Bhai, another one in the day, I am all for it, should I go ahead?". "You've screwed yourself up royally Aslam. Give Mushi a burial, then go home and pray. Wait for my call. I cannot take chances now"; Jadhav retorted. Aslam wanted to tell Jadhav that he was all up for the second kill but knew it would be suicidal to argue with Jadhav right now.

Aslam reached home after handing over Mushi's body to his trusted contact at the graveyard. He was still puzzled over the two calls and the actions they resulted in. He felt deeply saddened by what had happened. He knew this could spell doom for his career. His wife and son were fast asleep. He opened the refrigerator and helped himself to a cola. Once sober, he put on the handset on his mobile phone and tuned in the radio playing some music from the yesteryears, a thing he often did to relax. He had to keep awake and wait for Jadhav's call.

The call never came. He waited for an agonizingly long hour but couldn't resist sleep any longer. He sneaked into the bed beside his wife. The old bed creaked loudly as if resisting his weight. His wife's sleep got disturbed and almost mechanically she let out the usual diatribe about Aslam's coming late, his responsibility to the family, disturbance to their time and schedule, and other worldly stuff. Once the outburst was over, she slipped back into deep slumber without batting an eyelid. This was normal for Aslam. The outburst reminded him of a superfast train he had seen passing a platform at a small station at full speed. The noise and the silence thereafter were almost similar. "Why doesn't anyone give me orders to shoot her for a change? I will do that for free", he sneered before dozing off.

When he woke up the next morning the house was already empty. His son was off to school and his wife to the neighbours for her daily dose of tattling. He wondered why Jadhav hadn't called him back. As he was getting ready, he got a call. It was Rehmat Bhai, Jadhav's supervisor and mentor.

"I want to meet you today, come alone", he ordered Aslam in a grave tone.

Aslam was almost shaking as he sat on the couch in front of Rehmat. His heart was pounding heavily. He felt it could lunge out of his mouth any moment. He knew his career in the gang was in jeopardy after the goof-up he had committed. He looked around to see if Jadhav was present, needing some moral support. Rehman surprisingly was very calm and offered Aslam tea. He sighed as he began, "Jadhav's dead! Kripal shot him when Jadhav went to get him yesterday. We got Kripal in the morning while he was trying to flee"; Rehmat said slowly as he sipped his tea.

Aslam could feel his hands getting numb.

"Jadhav had called me yesterday night informing me that your son met with an accident in the night and hence you couldn't execute the task. He told me he would take care of it"; Rehmat continued.

"Surprisingly Mushi is missing as well. I don't know what's happening. I have lost two of my best men in a night!". Aslam froze, not understanding where this was going. A melee of thoughts agonized his mind. He decided to keep mum and let things take their course.

"Jadhav spoke highly of you. And that's why I had given you this chance. I have a shortage of men currently Aslam. I have orders to get a banker out tomorrow. Are you up for it?", Rehmat said placing his hand on Aslam's shoulders.

As Aslam was leaving, Rehmat said softly, "We are crooks but family matters to us as well! I hope your son is doing well. Take good care of him". Aslam nodded.

As soon as his son returned from school Aslam hugged him and wrapped a bandage around his head. He whispered something in his ears handing him a bar of big chocolate. Ayaan smiled gleefully.

A year later, Aslam was given a choice by Rehmat to take his family on an all-expenses-paid excursion to a foreign land of his choice in Asia. In the year that had passed Aslam had wooed everyone in the gang due to his almost indifferent nature in executing crimes and his eagerness to grow. He executed some of the most important assignments for his group that year. After the incident of the phone call mix-up, Aslam had researched and realized that the fake call was from Japan and the real one, the second call, as expected from China. He had considered many a time about calling up the Japan number and investigating the matter but something told him not to go after buried skeletons especially when no one knew about the episode. After all, that call had made him what he was today.

His choice of the country for the vacation was therefore obvious.

Aslam gazed out of the window. Ayaan jumped in joy beside him as he saw a train passing by.

Aslam smiled. "Do you know it does not have a driver, it's automatic!", he informed his son whose eyes widened in amazement looking at the Yurikamome gather pace on its tracks.

They had just checked into their small but comfortable room in a hotel in Tokyo overlooking the Odaiba bay.

He glanced around the room and picked up the house phone to order some tea, tired after his long flight from India. "Hello", he said gleefully as he heard the clicking sound of the phone being picked up.

A lady on the other side of the phone replied, "Moshi, Moshi, room service, how may I help you?"

4

WILDFIRE

At first, it looked like a series of orange luminescent street lights that Jishnu had seen when he had visited his grandfather's small-town last year, the ones that were hardly visible these days in Delhi, where he lived. Sitting in the back seat of the taxi that wound its way up the hills through the dark roads, he strained his eyes to get a better look. It cannot be street lights, its spread is a bit wider, and it's contiguous, he thought. And is that…is that smoke around it? Jishnu cried aloud, "Dad, look, fire!".

Jishnu's father, Rishi Mehta, who had dozed off in the front seat, was startled. "Jishnu, what?"; he cried as if caught stealing. Namrata, Jishnu's mother, came to life as well. The driver, Prabhu, smiled feebly, almost to himself. It had been a long day for the family. They had started early morning from their house in east Delhi, catching a train to Kathgodam to head for their vacation in the Kumaon mountains. The superfast train which usually took around 5 hours to reach its destination took almost double, thanks to a route diversion due to an accident. They reached Kathgodam, in the foothills of the Himalayas, around evening and were greeted by Prabhu, the driver of the taxi they had hired for the next 5 days.

They had planned to reach Ranikhet by the evening to enjoy the sunset, however, due to the delayed train, they had already lost half a day in their short plan. Rishi was concerned about a taxi ride in the hills after sunset. He had been admonished by his well-wishers umpteen times to plan his excursions in the hills during daylight. "It's not safe to drive in the dark on those tricky roads", everyone had said.

"That's not exactly the case", Prabhu had clarified when they started. "We prefer not to drive at night for reasons other than road accidents", he stated. "In fact, it's easier to drive at night since you can see the lights of an oncoming vehicle from a distance". Given the way he had been driving effortlessly since the past two hours, it seemed Prabhu was right.

Rishi glanced out of the car's window and saw the reason for Jishnu's excitement. A long streak of wildfire was winding up the hills, glowing in the dark. Its expanse did not look threatening though. It evoked a mixed feeling in Rishi, the sight was beautiful, yet ominous. The yellow and orange flares wound around the dark forest. It seemed like a necklace of fire around the neck of Ma Kaali, the goddess of destruction.

Jishnu had a different view, "It seems like a big dragon, flying over the mountains, has spewed fire to destroy the evil spirits here". "It's just wildfire Jishnu", the ever so practical Namrata couldn't help but deflate his flight of fantasy. "Pretty common in hills during these times", she stated matter-of-factly. "Sometimes it's created by design as well, to provide a gap in the forest so that accidental wildfires do not spread. It's called a fire line in that case".

"So, which one is this?"; the ever-curious Jishnu, all of ten years of age, wanted more.

"Ask Dad", Namrata ducked the question and pulled out her phone. The signal seemed weak but enough to continue the online chats with her friends back home, giving them each detail about the heavily planned family vacation.

Rishi was already mulling over his answer, not sure himself. When the question didn't pop up for a while he turned back and glanced at Jishnu. The boy was busy with his phone. After moments of frantic tapping, typing, and swiping at his smartphone, Jishnu finally announced, "This one seems like a fire line, looking at its symmetry and spread!"

The halt at Ranikhet was brief. The Mehta family spent a night there and, the very next morning headed to their next destination: Binsar, to keep the rest of the vacation plan on track. Prabhu stopped the car barely five minutes into the journey. Rishi could see a small temple in front of him. "Good to take blessings, first thing in the morning, from the goddess. This is an important temple here", and before they could say anything he stepped out of the car and entered the temple premises in a hurry. Rishi and Namrata looked at each other and sighed, then slowly got out of the taxi. Jishnu followed reluctantly still puzzled and frantically searching for the details of the spot they had stopped. It did not appear on his travel itinerary.

After a quick visit to the temple, the Mehtas stepped out and reached back to the taxi only to find Prabhu missing. Rishi glanced around as more cars with more tourists stopped near them. The car was unlocked so Namrata got in while Rishi and Jishnu went out in search of the driver. They found him a few feet down the road, smoking a beedi under a tree. "Prabhu, we are ready to leave", Rishi said softly. Prabhu smiled, threw the still burning stubble of the beedi onto the ground, and rushed towards him. Jishnu couldn't resist watching the half-lit beedi stub smoulder on the ground and wither out.

Hardly had they gone a few kilometres ahead, that Prabhu stopped the taxi again. The Mehtas looked up from their cell phones, almost mildly jolted by the halt. Rishi glanced around. They seemed to be in a military area looking at the signboards around. He looked at Prabhu quizzically. Prabhu pointed them to another temple in the front, hidden by the trees. "Another famous spot. It's where all the soldiers come to pray when they arrive at or depart from their posting. Very important here, must see!". Jishnu almost let out a cry of desperation, "I am not coming!". By the time Rishi could say something, Prabhu was out of the car and galloping towards the trees nearby. Rishi got out of the car. Namrata followed him slowly. As their eyes met, Rishi could feel the rage in her stare. "Will you set the driver's priorities right or want me to say it in my style, which I'm sure you won't like". "Well, we just started, I think it will be fine as we pull out of this area. Come let's have a quick look inside", Rishi replied sheepishly.

Namrata chose to stay back near the car, stretching her legs and making full use of the strong mobile signal in the area. She had to report this slow start of the day to her online friends.

Rishi killed some time in the non-descript temple, alone, with not a soul in sight. They had now seen five temples in their journey so far on Prabhu's insistence, three on the way up to Ranikhet the day before. He knew he needed to make Prabhu aware of their priorities; he just wanted an opportune moment. Religion is such a sensitive subject that you never know when you will offend someone with your practical thought, he felt.

"So, what next Prabhu ji? Is there any tourist spot that falls en-route our trip to Binsar", Rishi initiated a casual conversation with Prabhu, as they started again. The two stoppages had set them back by an hour already. "Well, there is a famous temple of a goddess that you can see. People here hold it in high regard", Prabhu said straight-faced. Rishi sighed. "Well let's not stop at any more temples, Prabhu Ji, except the ancient one that I told you about in the upper hills. We are here to see the mountains", Rishi stated pleasantly, wanting to keep the atmosphere cordial. Prabhu was expectedly silent for some time. "What else is there in the hills to see except these temples' sir, but as you say. You tell me where to stop".

The next few hours were spent silently. The taxi wound its way through the mountains, presenting splendid green vistas to marvel at. The Mehtas rolled down the car's windows and let the fresh breeze of the mountains surround them. The woody smell of the forest accentuated by the distinct fragrance of the palm trees gave them enough reason to breathe deep and relax. They only stopped once to have their favourite instant noodles at a roadside stall, wanting to keep the target to reach the resort at Binsar before evening.

The roads were now winding steeply and the forest around was thickening. Rishi sensed a change in the air. He sniffed heavily to ascertain the cause. Jishnu could feel something too. "Where is the burning smell coming from dad?". Rishi realized that's what his brain was searching for. The smell was of burnt wood. Straining his eyes, he could see ashes around the edges of the road and burnt wood too. "Seems like the jungle fire had come this way too"; Prabhu said nonchalantly, breaking his silence after a long time. "This seems recent"; Rishi muttered, concentrating on the road's sides. As the car climbed the hills further, things turned serious. Rishi could see some of the smaller trees by the road all burnt down. Some trees where just the stumps were left, could still be seen smouldering. They could see smoke around now. "Is it safe to go further?", a worried Rishi asked Prabhu. Prabhu did not seem bothered. Jishnu was fully excited now, almost hanging out from the window of the car. The furore caused Namrata to look up from her virtual world. Although the mobile connection was intermittent, she was still preparing all her photos and write-ups to be ready to post as soon as it was available again. She wanted to make sure that all that she laid her eyes upon on this vacation should fill the annals of her online existence. But as she glanced out of the window at the smouldering trees around, she suddenly felt jittery. The scene around was not to her comfort.

The car moved on, albeit a bit slowly now. Prabhu could sense the smoke increasing and the heat from the smouldering trees around both sides of the road could be felt on the skin. It was now Namrata's turn to ask, "Is it safe to go ahead, what if we get caught?". "Madam, this happens in hills sometimes, nothing to worry about, I have been in these situations before. The fire will not cross the road, rather cannot, due to the concrete. I will drive in the centre of the road, thankfully it's broad enough here, so don't worry", Prabhu was back to his courteous self now. What was common for Prabhu, was a rare experience for the family who was more used to be stuck in manmade disasters like bad traffic or killer smog. The wrath of the elements was something that they had never really experienced. So Prabhu's soothing words didn't provide the comfort that they were looking for. The smoke got heavier, and Prabhu rolled up all the windows. Rishi could see why. The trees at the edges of the road could now be seen on fire.

There was no wind thankfully and hence no flames leaping across the metallic road that served as a deterrent to the fire spreading upwards. Everyone was silent. Jishnu was excited and was filming the drive on his cell phone. Namrata was scared, to say the least, and her mind went numb. So numb that she didn't even think about capturing this once-in-a-lifetime moment of driving through fire.

The drive through the wildfire lasted for just about a minute, and it seemed it had never happened as soon as they were out of it. The bad patch was gone and Prabhu was again speeding towards their destination.

"Wildfires happen here almost every year", Prateek Bisht, the well-dressed manager of the resort explained the Mehtas as they sat at the dinner table. "They can occur naturally through excessive heat or friction in the densely populated jungles here. The pine trees here, which add to the beauty and provide such a lovely fragrance to the air, are highly flammable. They aid the rapid spread of the fire", the manager, a polished educated gentleman from Nainital, continued. The resort was not much occupied that season, the news of the rapidly spreading wildfires had reached the cities, and many concerned holidayers had cancelled their reservations. That gave Prateek ample time to give individual attention to each of his guests. Jishnu who had been listening intently to Prateek's explanation, interrupted, "But uncle, I have read that there are some notorious characters that do this on purpose as well". Prateek smiled back gently. "You are an intelligent little boy. Unfortunate as it is, this is a fact as well. Most of the trouble since the last few years is man-made. Some people light up small fires intentionally in the hills, few of which end up becoming large spread wildfires destroying hundreds, sometimes thousands of hectares of land. The exact reasons for the fires are mostly never known".

"But what do they get out of this?", Namrata asked innocently. "Money…land", Prateek explained, shrugging his shoulders. "Burn the area, leave it for some days then occupy it illegally for constructing houses or farms, sell the timber that you get as well. Some honey and Sal teak collectors do it for scaring away wild animals. Reasons might wary, but it's all for their selfish advantage". Prateek got up from his chair, "I'll take your leave now. Don't forget to try the rasmalai and banana pudding. Chef's special! And don't worry about the calories, we will go on a hike in the hills tomorrow early morning!". "Why don't we punish such people? We should just blast them with dynamite", Jishnu exploded, still engaged with the topic. "There are laws and police are getting serious now. Google it up and I will test your knowledge tomorrow", Prateek waved Jishnu a goodbye and moved to the other tables.

~ * ~

The next morning, Jishnu was wandering about the resort, his parents still trying to get ready to be in time for the hike to the Zero Point, from where, as Prateek had mentioned, you could get a brilliant 180-degree view of the Himalayas. "Weather permitting"; had been his disclaimer. Jishnu looked at his watch and wished his parents could be out in time. He pulled out his mobile phone and started clicking photographs of the beautiful cottages of the resort that blended harmoniously with the green hills. He then pointed the lens at the magnificent green hills that were visible all around from the resort's garden. He moved about the garden away from the hotel's reception lobby which was supposed to be the meeting point for the morning trek. He reached a fence that overlooked a small road that passed behind the resort. The view of the winding deserted road, canopied by pine trees and surrounded by beautiful shrubs and flowering plants, was an artistic view for a city dweller like Jishnu, who had never seen a road devoid of traffic. Jishnu slid behind a huge tree, partly to give himself support and partly to provide a background to his photo, a trick he had learned in an online photography workshop. He zoomed in and out in his display to look for the best shot. His eyes suddenly caught a movement in the frame, and as he zoomed in, he could see a few boys down the valley on the other side of the road struggling with something. Inquisitive, Jishnu used his high-end phone camera and zoomed in to look at the boys. There were two boys, one having a lanky figure, who looked to be around fifteen and the other a stout boy smaller in age, probably nearly as old as Jishnu. As Jishnu adjusted his camera to see the object that they were struggling with, his heart skipped a beat. There was a small fire near their feet. The younger boy looked around and threw dry leaves into the fire from a bag he carried and the other poured some liquid on it from a bottle. Jishnu realized that they were building a fire. He sensed that the boys had nefarious intent. He dashed along the resort's boundary towards a gate from where a small flight of stairs ran downward leading to the road. Fuelled by a sense of adventure, his moves practiced umpteen times in ambush games that he was a champion at, in no time Jishnu was near the edge of the road from where he could get a clear look at the boys. To his reassurance, the fire hadn't picked up pace and the two boys were frantically trying to fuel it. They were clumsily trying to heave the dry leaves spread around into the fire which was cutting out the fire rather than build it. The boys were hardly thirty to forty feet down the slope from the edge of the road, unaware of Jishnu's presence, committed to the task at hand. "Hey, stop that!", Jishnu shouted. The boys froze and looked up, terror-stricken. "Douse that fire or I will call the police", he said pointing to his mobile phone. The boys looked at each other, the younger one started to run away but the other one grabbed him by the collar. "He's seen us, running will not solve the problem", he muttered. "What do we do now Pappu"; the younger one stammered. "We were just trying to put out the fire, no wrongdoing intended"; Pappu shouted back to Jishnu. "Oh no, you were not! Douse the fire now or I will use my phone. I have even captured your pictures here". Now Pappu was worried. He nodded and started hitting the fire with his slippers. His partner Bablu too took the cue and started dousing the small fire with a gunny sack they had with them. Jishnu elated by his victory shouted, "Quick, faster". He did not realize in his excitement that he had come dangerously close to the edge of the road. His next step made him tumble down the slope, towards the boys, like a juggernaut. Pappu and Bablu were not prepared for this. They saw Jishnu roll down, hitting the shrubs and crushing the foliage around. Jishnu tried to regain control, desperately trying to grab on to a support. He got his hands onto the trunk of a small tree, but slipped again, his shoulders hitting against a small rock. He cried in pain and his hands numbed for a moment. He fell a few feet more and then as if by magic, his legs got stuck in a tree's roots and he stopped. He pulled himself up and rested by the trunk of the tree, his shoulder in pain. He felt a bit dizzy. Pappu and Bablu, who had been successful in dousing the small fire, looked at Jishnu intently. Bablu blurted; "I am afraid Pappu. I don't want to get beaten by the police". Pappu slapped Bablu's shoulders, lightly chiding him, "Shut Up, I will handle it". And before Bablu could react Pappu rushed towards the spot where Jishnu lay, the gunny bag in his hands.

Jishnu saw the tall boy coming at him and struggled to get up on his feet. He had partly managed to regain his ground, when Pappu pounded on him, covering his head, shoulders, and chest with the gunny bag. Jishnu slumped to the ground. Bablu was at Pappu's heels in no time. "Well done", he said smiling. But his smile did not last long as a struggling Jishnu's leg hit his stomach. Bablu slumped to the ground writhing in pain. "Get up you squirrel, show some fight, we need to tie his hands. Give me that cotton bag you have". Bablu was still in pain, but Pappu's call to his manhood made him get up somehow as he handed over the bag. Pappu overpowered Jishnu and used the loops of the cotton bag to tie his hands. Then he stepped back and asked Bablu to do the same. Jishnu was shouting and throwing his legs around. His sound was muffled by the gunny bag but could still be heard. "Let's take his mobile phone and leave"; Pappu said. They approached Jishnu and as Pappu held him Bablu searched his pockets. There was nothing there. They stepped back again. "He had it in his hands when he fell, must be somewhere here, search", commanded Pappu. Jishnu was yelling curses now, the ones his father and mother had told him never to use. As the boys stepped away searching for his phone, Jishnu stopped his bickering. He suddenly felt afraid with no one around, unable to see anything. "Hey where did you guys go, come back" he shouted, but no response. Meanwhile, Bablu's search yielded results when he found the mobile lying near the undergrowth. "I found it"; he shouted. Pappu ran to him and patted him for his success. "Let's get going now". Jishnu heard him and shouted, "Hey, you can't leave me like this, my parents will come here soon looking for me. I will tell them everything. Release me now". Bablu stopped in his tracks. Pappu who was holding Bablu's hand dragging him along, had to stop too. "He's seen us, what if he tells the police, we will be in trouble", Bablu spoke softly. "So, what do you suggest we do, Mr. Genius. Kill him, bury him, torch him?", Pappu retorted. "Let's take him along with us", Bablu suggested. "Are you out of your mind, what do we do with him then, we can't just take him home, make him have lunch, and wish he will forgive and forget everything just like that!", Pappu cried out. "Who said that you tall blockhead", Bablu quipped. "We can use the old log cabin of the Bhoot Bangla (haunted house), it's walkable from here and not easy to find as well". The tables were turning, Pappu who was in the lead in all the action till now, was beginning to see the logic in his younger partner's plan. In their innumerous earlier escapades together, Bablu had provided some great lifesaving ideas. Pappu was sorted. "And then what?", he questioned.

"To be frank, I don't know, but we will have time to sort this out", Bablu said candidly. "Okay, let's do it", Pappu said sounding convinced. "Play along with me", he started walking back towards Jishnu.

Bablu saw Pappu looking for something on the ground as he neared Jishnu. He picked up a sharp piece of wood before initiating a dialogue with his soon-to-be captive. "You are right, we can't leave you here! Not because we fear the police or anyone else, they are all in our pockets. Rather because I can sense some dangerous animals loitering around. And I don't want them to have a helpless child for lunch".

Jishnu was frightened, "What animals, I know there are no tigers around here, do you mean leopards? But they don't attack, don't try to fool me, I know everything". "Well there are leopards, and then there are others. I don't know what might come but I sense something". Pappu waved to Bablu and signalled him. Bablu was dazed at first but then understood the context. He was a master at mimicking animals' and birds' voices. He stared with his favourite, the hoot of an owl. They heard it all right, Jishnu and Pappu, and it was brilliantly done. But it did not leave the desired effect on the hostage. Pappu gave a long stare to Bablu and waved his hands in the form of a paw, to signal him to get to something more gruesome. Bablu got the cue, the next growl that emanated from his throat did shake up Jishnu. It was perfectly pitched, not loud enough, and somewhere between the growl of a leopard and a bear, but it did the trick. Jishnu started throwing his feet to stand up. "You heard that? Something's near. I will get you to safety. Now, just take my hand and no smartness". The one thing that Jishnu wanted desperately was to get up and be on his feet so he accepted the offer gladly. Once on his feet, he contemplated whether he should comply with the boy's wishes or make a dash. He had lost the sense of direction, and could only see light and very hazy figures as the gunny bag still covered his eyes and face. As if reading his mind, he heard Pappu shout to Bablu, "Hey, give me your pocket knife". Bablu looked at him quizzically. "What knife is he talking about?", he thought. And then he saw Pappu move around in a funny fashion rustling up the leaves around him, not moving more than a few inches though. "Thanks for that, isn't this the one we killed the wild boar with?", he pretended to laugh. Bablu got it now, as he saw Pappu pull out the sharp wood that he had collected earlier from the ground. "He's overacting though!", he thought.

"Hey, hey, no need for the knife, I am a friendly person. Let's talk this over", Jishnu stuttered. Pappu was glad it was going his way. "Just follow my instructions and walk along with us, no smartness", he roared, trying to sound authoritative. "Go where with you?", replied Jishnu, concern ringing through his tone. Pappu thrust his make-believe knife into Jishnu's back and prodded him to move. "You want to be left here to be eaten by that beast that's approaching? Just move now", Pappu roared again and waved to Bablu to lead Jishnu forward. Bablu grabbed hold of Jishnu's hand and they started their journey to the log cabin.

Jishnu was scared now, he did not know how to get out of the situation. He couldn't see anything clearly and his hands continued to be tied so there was no way he could run without removing the gunny bag blocking his vision. He also had the presence of that animal that he had heard in his mind. He knew the only way out from here was to talk his way through it. "Guys, listen, why don't you just let me go and I will not tell anything to anyone. I promise", Jishnu tried to engage them as they walked silently through a path that seemed to go downhill, but wasn't that hard to tread. Bablu glanced at Pappu, but Pappu gestured him to keep on moving. He just prodded Jishnu forward by pressing the pointed end of the stick a bit into his back. Jishnu winced and blurted, "Ok alright, I will not speak any further, sorry brother!".

~ * ~

They reached the log cabin after a 15-minute walk, mostly in silence, except when Bablu practiced his bird calls and once a growl at the behest of Pappu, to keep Jishnu's fear alive. The log cabin which was still in good shape stood in front of a big bungalow in an area surrounded by huge trees.

Like many folklores that teemed the region, this bungalow had been termed haunted by the villagers around. There were many stories around the bungalow which was at least fifty to sixty years old. The stories around the sightings of various ghastly figures near the property had resulted in not arousing the fancy of any buyer over the years, and hence it continued to lay in ruins. The log hut stood not more than three hundred meters from the bungalow. Pappu and Bablu had frequented the log hut for the past many years to avoid people when they had gotten into trouble over their wayward activities. They had never experienced anything except extreme calm and peace here. No one ever approached anywhere near the bungalow, not even any unlawful and antisocial elements. It seemed they always had the place to themselves and a lot of birds and small animals of the jungle.

They rested Jishnu on a squeaky, bit broken but comfortable wooden chair inside the log hut. "I need some water to drink", Jishnu said softly breaking his silence. "These city dwellers I tell you! We barely walked 15-20 minutes and look at him, he's already thirsty", Pappu swore under his breath. Bablu waved to him in reassurance and turned to Jishnu. "There's only water in a bucket here from the monsoon, three months back. It's a bit greenish though, you want that or it can wait?", he said sarcastically. Jishnu surrendered again, "I can wait, surely". "Good, now we are stepping out into the porch for a few minutes, we need to talk. You behave yourself and stay quiet. Else our big fellow is still carrying that knife. Besides we are now in front of the Bhoot Bangla here. You don't want to conjure up some blood-sucking restless spirit, do you?", Bablu made his point and stepped outside. Pappu followed.

Bablu sat at the wooden steps to the log hut, a smile on his face, as he watched Pappu rolling on the ground with laughter that he was trying to suppress desperately. The ground was covered with tall, untamed grass which was rubbing its colour onto Bablu's white shirt, but he hardly seemed to care. "You gave it to that guy in there, you little devil. He's really scared I can assure you".

Bablu laughed a little too. "Now what do we do with him? We must think fast! People would surely be looking for him now", he said settling down after a while.

The Mehtas had indeed started the search for their missing child. They spent the first fifteen to twenty minutes going around the resort looking for Jishnu themselves. After that, they started involving the hotel staff, and after another fifteen minutes of futile search, they raised the official alarm. It had now been almost an hour and a half since then but he was nowhere to be seen. Prateek, the hotel's manager, had informed the police over the telephone but they had still not reached, since the nearest police post was about twenty kilometres downhill. Prateek meanwhile had instructed a few of his staff to start searching outside of the hotel as well, in case Jishnu had just wandered off to catch some sights.

Namrata was panicking. She was trying to call Jishnu's number but it was out of range. Rishi tried to console her. "He will be around somewhere, we will find him soon!", he kept repeating, sounding unconvinced himself. "He's a smart, clever child and a responsible one at that. He's not simply wandered off. It's something else. Where's the police?", Namrata retorted.

~ * ~

Bablu and Pappu were scratching their heads. They had been partners in crime on a lot of occasions and most of the time had got through unscathed from tricky situations using their sharp minds, especially Bablu's. Pappu and Bablu had known each other for the last three years. They both lived in the same village, further down the hills. They went to the same school and got thrown out of the school at the same time. The commonalities didn't end here. Both boys lived with their grandparents. Pappu's parents worked in the nearby city as daily wagers leaving Pappu at the mercy of his grandfather, a desperate drunkard who cared about nothing but his next bottle of alcohol. And Bablu's parents had died in the cholera pandemic that had hit the village a few years back. He had a doting set of grandparents, but unfortunately, they had neither the means nor the strength to feed the three of them. The circumstances had swerved both boys to become boisterous, regularly getting into trouble with everyone. What started as fun and acts of rebellion, soon turned into activities that just fell short of petty crimes. They had been caught and reprimanded several times for stealing eatables from the grocery stores in the village. They had been beaten by the guards at the government-run local school for trying to disrupt classes and harass the teachers, even after they had been long rusticated. They were infamous for stealing fruits and vegetables from the farms. At first, the villagers had left them off with gentle warnings understanding their plight and sympathizing with them. However, things got serious recently when some villagers caught the boys selling some of the stolen fruits in the neighbouring village's market to make money. The villagers escalated the matter to Ram Nath, the policeman who lived in the village. Ram Nath had a serious talk with Pappu and Bablu, warning them of serious consequences if they did not mend their ways. He admonished them that he would keenly watch them and would not mind sending them to the nearest detention centre if they continued the nuisance. The boys had no choice but to mend their ways and control their urge to create mischief. Things were going well, until yesterday when a stranger approached them, asking them to perform a small task for him. The small task, easy as it seemed, made them land in the mess they were in now.

Jishnu could hear the boys talking, although their voices weren't mostly clear he could make out that the context was his captivity. He had been sitting patiently till now but the sack on his face was now suffocating him. "Hey guys, you need to get this thing off me, I am feeling breathless", he shouted. Pappu and Bablu came rushing in. Bablu spoke in his usual harsh tone, "You are a demanding wretch! Don't you think your foolish utterances might make us harm you". But now Jishnu had also decided to persist. He knew even captives had their rights. He had seen enough television to understand that opening a conversation helped and demanding what was necessary was usually a good place to start. "Well, I could anyway die if I continued to wear this sack around my head. I can't breathe properly ", he retorted. Bablu was taken aback by this sudden counter-attack. He took off the sack from Jishnu's head in anger and put it over his face. "You liar, it's perfectly fine in here. I can breathe freely", he shouted again. Pappu entered the log hut, curious about the noise around, and was surprised to see Jishnu staring at Bablu, who was fiddling with the sack around his head. Pappu sighed and rushed to Bablu's side. "I have already seen both of you earlier, and now once again, so what's the use of this face cover?", Jishnu said cautiously. "What do you guys want?".

Pappu pulled off the sack from Bablu's head and glared at him as their eyes met. Bablu realized the stupidity of his act. "He has a point"; he said sheepishly addressing Pappu. "Of course, he does"; Pappu said gritting his teeth. "Maybe we should also free up his hands, since he has already seen us, and maybe even drop him home. Maybe he will ask us in and make him meet his parents, even ask us for tea and share a few biscuits", Pappu mocked. Jishnu smiled, barely controlling his laughter. Bablu frowned and walked out. Pappu followed.

"These city dwellers are weak. He will fall sick if we keep him tied up and don't provide him with food and water. You said we could think of a plan when we get here. Where's your plan?", Pappu said pacing up and down the verandah of the log hut. Bablu was thinking hard. He knew there was no easy solution to this. They were in deep trouble. "If only you had listened to me when I told you not to fall for that strange man's offer. And now you want me to bail us out of this situation?", Bablu addressed Pappu, frustrated. Pappu was aghast. He turned around and started looking for an object to throw at Bablu. Bablu had spent enough time with Pappu to know what was coming. He ran inside the log hut. Barely had he managed to get inside that a slipper came flying in missing him by a whisker. He ran and hid behind the chair on which Jishnu was sitting. Jishnu panicked on the sudden movement around and stood upon an impulse. He suddenly realized he was not tied to the chair and that the door was open. He dashed towards the door, only to run into Pappu who was entering, the other slipper in his hand. On an impulse, Jishnu retracted and ran back towards the chair again. The second flying slipper followed, hitting him on the hand and then bouncing off to hit Bablu's face which was peeping from behind the chair. Jishnu fell on the ground, losing balance. Pappu stood at the door, looking at both the boys, one rubbing his face and the other lying flat on the floor. "This is unfair", Pappu shouted back at Bablu. "You had agreed to the plan. Wouldn't you share the money that we would have got eventually?". Bablu had always feared Pappu's temper. He knew he had to cajole him and calm him down. "I did, when did I say something else. But this didn't sound right to both of us, right? You were also sceptical, weren't you? Now come on, relax, we will handle it. Think of the money, we will not get it if you behave like this". Jishnu sat up straight "Are you guys planning to ask for a ransom? My father's business isn't doing well for your information. But I can give you my tab if you let me go". Pappu looked at Jishnu in disbelief. "Do we look like kidnappers to you, you little brat". "And what money are you talking about, you stupid dwarf?", he addressed Bablu. "Remember the place had to be burnt down properly for us to receive the money. Thanks to this wretched boy here the only thing we burned is a few twigs. And as it stands, we now have to give back the advance which we happily spent yesterday on the chicken curry".

Bablu knew Pappu was right. He gathered courage and stood up. "Let's think it over, big guy. Calm down", he said easing into the chair on which Jishnu had been sitting a while back.

Pappu locked the door behind him, still standing guard on the door. Jishnu sat on the floor puzzled. Pappu's diatribe had revealed a lot of information. It was scattered and Jishnu's deft brain was trying to piece it all together. "But why would someone give you money to burn down trees", he thought out aloud. It was now Bablu's turn to give Pappu a mean stare. Pappu's expressions changed as he realized he had spilled the beans. At least some of it.

~ * ~

It was just yesterday morning that Pappu and Bablu had met a young man on their way to the small river, where they liked to bathe and rest, virtually killing time till lunch. The man, stylishly dressed with long curly locks and sporting flashy sunglasses, stopped them. He was there to meet them, he told, and that he had been referred to them by someone in the neighbouring village. "Who?", Pappu had inquired, rather sceptically. "Chandu, Chand Prakash. He said he knew you well and that you two were the best in the region to help me out!". Chandu was indeed a friend, or rather a partner in crime. When the boys stole groceries, vegetables, and fruit from their village, it was Chandu who directed them to the appropriate neighbouring villages or cities to sell it, and many times also shielded them from getting caught. Chandu was a bit older than Pappu and had visited the police station multiple times due to his exploits. He was a jovial person to be with but his company usually meant trouble. So, after the recent admonishment by police officer Ram Nath, Pappu and Bablu had decided to stay away from him, for their good.

The man minced no words in his offer. He wanted a specific area beside the road leading to the entrance of the various resorts nearby to be burned down. He stated matter-of-factly that he wanted to build a small shop there, and could get through the approvals easily by bribing his way. He just needed a clear piece of land. "Why don't you do it yourself?", Bablu had enquired. "Well, too risky for me, if someone sees me. I am to run the shop later you see. And I live far away from here, so I can't wait and watch for the opportune moment. You guys are local kids, no one will even bat an eye even if they see you. They will think you are playing. And it should be very quick. There's been a lot of wildfire around anyway. It had reached downhill a few days back but died. The wood is still smouldering in some parts. It's very easy to pass this away as an extension of the same wildfire. No one will even raise an eyebrow".

The man's offer to pay them hard cash in return was handsome by the boys' standard. They knew the money could easily fetch them their needs for a year. Pappu was excited. Bablu was cautious. He knew they were getting into something potentially dangerous. He pulled Pappu back and murmured his reservations. Pappu tried to reason with Bablu, about how easy it was if they used their minds. They had created fires a lot of times in their villages to scare away the animals. This was no different. Bablu sensed danger. "It could spread, how will we control it and limit it to the area he wants to get cleared".

"Oh, I have thought about it already, the fire will self-contain", the man spoke loudly, having heard them. "It's a very sweet spot surrounded by a road on three sides and rocks on the rest. A small piece of land tucked between the wide winding road". He moved his hands and arms around to explain. Bablu was still hesitant. "Oh, and by the way, did I mention you get a mobile as well for doing this. Chandu had mentioned that the little one was crazy about mobiles. He had assured me you would want that".

~ * ~

"We have his mobile, we can keep it and let him go", Bablu broke the silence. "What? I knew it's been only about the mobile for you all along", Pappu glared at him. "Oh, come on...", Bablu retorted. "He knows the situation and would understand we didn't mean any harm; we don't want to create further mess". "And he will simply forgive and forget, just like that", Pappu retorted. Jishnu jumped on the opportunity he was looking for, "Of course, I would, if it's not your fault". "You better be quiet, this is all because of you anyway", Pappu gave Jishnu a piece of his mind. The three of them went silent. The wind blowing through the hills could be heard through the small window in the log house. Pappu glanced at his watch. 9 am, almost three hours had passed since this trouble had started. He knew somewhere in his mind that the police would have arrived by now, and they could be in trouble.

"We need to shift base first", he addressed Bablu. "Let's go inside the Bhoot Bangla"; he continued. "At least no one will dare come inside". "So, there is actually a haunted house here, whoa!"; Jishnu blabbered, unable to control his excitement. "Yes, dumbo, and we are already in its courtyard", Pappu replied tersely. "Are you serious Pappu? We have never been inside, it's spooky if you ask me", Bablu chimed in. "To be precise, it's you who hasn't been inside. I have, multiple times, without you, even at night once. There's nothing spooky inside except a black mean cat who could tolerate both of you if you do as I say. I have built a rather sound relationship with him by now".

"I am so for it; I need to be inside a haunted house. Let's go"; Jishnu was upon his feet. Pappu and Bablu stared at their captive in disbelief.

~ * ~

They entered the large wooden bungalow through a door at the back. The journey to the back door through the wild, untamed grass and the occasional cobweb, did give Jishnu the adrenalin rush. The door made the mandatory creaking sound and the atmosphere, as they entered a large living room, was definitely eerie. So, what they showed in the horror movies is true, Jishnu thought. It does look like this. Bablu was a bit afraid too to start with but gained his confidence back looking at Pappu who deftly led them through the house. Bablu knew his partner and if he had said it was safe, he knew there was nothing to worry about.

Bablu led them to a small room where lay a small wooden table and a few creaking chairs. The table was placed in front of a broad window overlooking the courtyard, a perfect position for them to see if anyone approached. "Sit, relax, we have this grand place all to ourselves. Beware of the spiders though they are not spirits, they can bite, the bigger ones", he smiled looking amused at the two pale faces in front of him. "Here, have these", he threw a banana each to Bablu and Jishnu that he took out of his bag.

Jishnu's hands were still tied. So, he missed the missile. Pappu laughed and signalled Bablu to untie Jishnu's hands. "What if he tries to run". "I can do that now as well, you have my hands tied not legs, remember!", Jishnu said sarcastically.

As they gobbled down the fruit, Jishnu looked around at the magnificent rooms visible from where he sat. The central room, where most rooms opened had a beautiful long table and some amazingly crafted cupboards lining the walls. Bablu's eyes were wandering as well although looking more for any movement or warning signs rather than admiring the beauty of the woodwork or rooms. Pappu finished his banana and looked carefully outside from the window. No sign of any movement. He relaxed and focused back on the two boys in front of him, who were leaning out of their seats in all directions to get better views of the house. "Well, since you both seem very interested, let me show you around my mansion", Pappu said in a royal tone.

Jishnu's fear of the unknown diminished as Pappu took them around the house. The rooms were spacious and airy and bright, thanks to the large windows, some of whose glasses were broken, letting fresh air in. The furniture was still in good shape although the beddings were either missing or torn badly.

There were definitely cobwebs all around, at many places wood from the walls and ceilings had caved in and there was grass that grew out from many of the cracks in the floors, but otherwise, the house looked nothing like a place a bunch of boys would be afraid of. Maybe things would be different in the night, Jishnu thought to himself. "Pappu, when did you come here all by yourself and why?", Bablu quizzed. "Well remember when you were down with fever a few months back, I used to meet Chandu pretty frequently then. He brought me here once. There have been stories about a treasure buried here, so Chandu wanted to have a look himself, just in case he got lucky". "Did he find anything?", Bablu questioned. "Just dug out holes and some cat shit! Even if there was something here, it would have been stolen years ago. This place has been declared haunted for decades; do you think the daredevils would have left anything. Now what's left are just stories of the owner's ghosts and these useless things lying around. Nothing that could earn us a fortune", Pappu replied shaking his head. "You could still make a decent sum if you sold some of this delicate crockery, the ones that are still intact. It would be difficult to drag this furniture anywhere; else they could fetch a price too. And by the way, the taps are all brass, they could sell too. These are all antiques that have a lot of demand in cities", Jishnu couldn't help throw in his advice. Pappu and Bablu stared at him. They were not sure whether Jishnu was in any way perturbed on being held captive.

Suddenly there was a loud sound of crockery falling in the central dining room, accompanied by a loud groan. Jishnu and Bablu froze in fear. Pappu laughed loudly. "Don't be scared you fools, that's Kaalu, the cat I talked about. Half the menace here which people are afraid of is created by him and his friends. He's a devil all right. Come I will introduce you guys to him", Pappu said and started walking towards the source of the sound. Jishnu and Bablu had no choice but to follow him. As they entered the dining room, they saw a huge black cat nudging at a big wild spider, perched atop one of the cupboards. As the cat saw the boys approaching, it fled through the nearest open window, pushing a small crockery plate in the process, that fell to the ground and shattered. "He certainly doesn't like you both", Pappu laughed.

"So, its Kaalu instead of the spirit whom passers-by have heard throwing the crockery in anger every now and then?", Bablu wondered aloud. "Maybe", Pappu shrugged his shoulders.

Jishnu slumped down at a chair nearby, his legs tired from all the walking since morning. "I want to know the time", he asked Pappu. Pappu stiffened as if coming out of a dream with a jolt. Suddenly, this simple question diffused the lively atmosphere that had been built in the last hour or so. Pappu glanced at his old watch. Another hour had passed. He surveyed the courtyard through the large windows. Not a soul in sight. He waved to Bablu to come near him. "You keep sitting there, and dare not move", he ordered Jishnu. Pappu took Bablu to a corner in the large room. "Strangely, the police haven't arrived yet looking for him", he told Bablu. "Maybe they have, but just haven't come to this side yet. The policemen fear this place as well, you know", Bablu reasoned. "I hear you but something tells me that's not the case. Anyway, what do we do now, we can't just hang in here with an abducted boy". Bablu was already thinking, his little but sharp mind already building permutations and combinations. Take the boy to the village with them and risk being calling kidnappers. Leave him here or somewhere else and risk being identified by him later. Drop him back at the hotel and possibly meet the same fate.

Throw him off a cliff! Bablu shook his head wildly, he knew he was going in the wrong direction. Pappu could see that his partner was having a hard time in coming up with options, he knew the situation was unlike anything they had ever been in before. They were just a bunch of rogue boys and deep down they were not comfortable with the situation. Somewhere Pappu also knew he shared the larger blame as Bablu wasn't too keen to take up this task in the first place. He patted Bablu and signalled him to take his time. He walked back slowly to Jishnu and pulled another chair to sit beside him.

"It's 10 am", he said softly pulling out a water bottle from the bag Bablu had carried and offering it to Jishnu. "Is this tap water? I am used to drinking filtered or mineral water", Jishnu said feebly. Pappu smiled sarcastically, "This water comes from streams originating from snow-capped mountains. It's so pure that some of your bottled water companies come here to take it away. It's safe, don't worry".

Jishnu was thirsty and it made sense to take the plunge. He sipped slowly at first and then before he knew it, he had downed half the bottle. It was indeed refreshing. "My parents would be worried, what's your plan?", Jishnu asked innocently. Pappu nodded his head in disbelief. A plan was exactly what they lacked. "Look, I know by now, at least a bit of what happened. I know it's not your fault. You can just drop me back, and I will make up a story. It's easy. I will delete your video from my mobile, so no proof", Jishnu got theatrical. Pappu had forgotten about the mobile. He glanced back at Bablu who got the hint and slowly pulled out the mobile from his pocket. "It's safe with me", he reassured.

"Well open it and delete the video he captured", Pappu ordered. Bablu fiddled with the mobile for a while. "It's locked and I cannot see the keypad", he said almost speaking to himself. "Tell him the PIN", Pappu ordered Jishnu. "There is no PIN, it's thumb print-based", Jishnu replied. "What, don't fool me! Just tell me the PIN". "There is no PIN. Look give it to me and I can unlock it for you". Pappu waved to Bablu who handed over the handset to Jishnu. They watched in wonder as the phone came to life by the mere touch of Jishnu's thumb. Bablu snatched it off Jishnu's hand as soon as the phone was unlocked. He meddled with it for a while before reaching the picture gallery. He played the last video capturing them lighting the fire. Bablu had a basic knowledge about the functions of a smartphone, having held some of the models from his friends in the neighbouring villages. But those had mostly been basic models or refurbished phones, which were prevalent in these areas. He had a keen interest in possessing one himself and thus Jishnu's latest high-end device that he held in his hand fascinated him. But he was largely clueless about how to use it. "Did you delete it", Pappu questioned. "Well, I ...", Bablu fumbled. "Don't tell me you don't know how to, have you been fooling me all the time saying you know how to handle a mobile?", Pappu roared. Pappu had no clue about how a mobile phone worked, and never cared much as well. He always wondered what people did on a mobile phone, straining their necks all day when they were not even calling anyone. Jishnu got up and peeped from behind Bablu. "Just click this dustbin button", he said softly. Pappu glared at Bablu. "I knew that ", Bablu glared in turn at Jishnu but clicked the button nevertheless to delete the file. "Done", Bablu smiled at Pappu victoriously. "Partially, I would say", Jishnu giggled. "It has to be deleted from the bin permanently. Thankfully there is no connection so it didn't go to the cloud where I could restore it from". The joke didn't go well with Pappu. "Now don't act over smart and throw terms at us. I can throwback ten others at you that you city boys won't be able to comprehend at all", he shouted. "Like what?", Jishnu was liking it. Pappu's brain, caught off-guard, fished for the options in his vocabulary. "Like Bhaat", he said after a while. "Oh, I know that one, I eat Dal-Bhaat all the time". Pappu grappled for something other, "Like Bal Mithai". "That's my father's favourite sweet, he's planning to buy a ton from Almora on our way back". "Like Arsa, like Singori", Bablu chimed in with force. "Ok I don't know those, but I can find out". "Like Laata", Bablu continued, sensing victory. "Now you are building words up". "No, I am not, you loser! Try Oija", Bablu continued to rub it in. "Oija, ha ha, that's a good one Bablu", Pappu laughed heartily. "I can find the meaning, give me a minute", Jishnu said hurriedly, not willing to give in. "And how may I ask?", Pappu mocked. "Ok Google, what is Oija", Jishnu shouted.

Pappu laughed at first but then froze as he heard a lady's voice. For the first time since they had entered the Bhoot Bangla he was scared. Bablu froze too but realized the voice was coming from the phone. Google assistant had just announced that it could not help as there was no data connection. "Ah, there is no network here else I would have told you. There's nothing I can't find via my phone". Pappu and Bablu were still staring at the phone wondering what happened. "Was that your mother?", Pappu asked feebly. "That was Google", Jishnu said in disbelief, "You've never Googled?". Pappu and Bablu stared at each other, not sure what to say. Jishnu sensed their discomfort. "It's okay, I can tell you about it, it's simple and useful. You can ask it anything and it answers back. We don't have a connection here but still if you give my phone back, I can show how the assistant works offline". Pappu grabbed Bablu who was moving ahead to hand the phone back to Jishnu.

"You think we are fools to believe your phone speaks. I am sure that was your mother ", Pappu mocked. Jishnu nodded his head in disbelief. "But how did he switch it on sitting there?", Pappu whispered to Bablu who seemed clueless as well. There was silence for a while. Jishnu slumped down in his chair suddenly. "My mother would be worried. No, in fact, my father would be more worried. My mother would probably be busier tweeting about me missing or uploading my retro pictures on Insta". Pappu slid nearer to Bablu and whispered, "This guy is from a different planet, it's no use keeping him with us, he's just trouble. Do you have a plan yet, or do we just run away from here?". The usually chatty Bablu too seemed lost for an answer.

~ * ~

Jishnu was suddenly filled with sadness, the child in him arching over the practical, brave boy that he was being till now. The drop in energy and change in his mood was evident for Pappu and Bablu to pick up. Pappu saw no way out of the situation. He knew they had to release the boy but feared the repercussions when the boy would spill the beans in front of his parents who would surely report to the police.

Pappu was deep in his thought when he heard Bablu shouting "Oija…". "Oh, come on Bablu, the game has ended, he couldn't answer that", Pappu sneered. Bablu continued excitedly "Oija…come here, see this!". Pappu rushed towards the broad window in the room to look at the subject of Bablu's excitement. His eyes widened as he saw two men standing near the opening in the woods that lead to the Bhoot Bangla. Both were waving their hands animatedly and intermittently pointing towards where Pappu and Bablu currently stood. Bablu ducked below the window and shouted to Pappu to do the same. "They are far off, they can't see us yet", Pappu said softly as he continued to stare at the two men. "One of them is the hotel manager, I recognize him, surely he would be knowing about the haunted house and wouldn't dare come closer", Pappu informed Bablu. Jishnu caught the commotion and peeped from behind. He instantly recognized the driver, Prabhu, and the resort manager Prateek. "Hey", Jishnu let out a shout of excitement impulsively and ran towards the backdoor from where they had entered. Pappu and Bablu rushed after him, but Jishnu had taken a sound lead. The moment he was out of the door, Pappu knew they had lost the battle. He held back Bablu. "We can't be seen by anyone, let him go, we anyway had to do that, there was no option". Bablu understood. They tiptoed to the window of the adjacent room which gave them more cover and looked outside. Jishnu had reached the two men and they were talking. He waved once or twice towards the log hut. The men looked around, discussed something, and then all three of them started walking away towards the trail that would join the road that lead to the resort. The boys saw Jishnu holding the manager's hand and walking away slowly. He glanced back once and then they all faded away in the distance.

~ * ~

Pappu and Bablu weighed their options. Staying in the Bhoot Bangla wasn't advisable. Even though everyone feared to tread near it, the boy had seen it and might lead the police to them. They could neither return to their village, the local police could identify them by the boy's description and would come straight to the village. They had the option of going to their friend Chandu in the neighbouring village. He had been in such situations a hundred times and could suggest a suitable plan of action. But then people in their village knew about their association and could lead the police to Chandu as well. They knew they had to disappear from the scene completely for some days. Pappu suggested they visit his aunt who lived in a small hamlet in the hills, away from their village. Pappu visited her once a year with his parents, but could surely make up a story for them turning up suddenly. She was an old lady, lonely and always welcoming. They could reach there by night if they hitched a ride soon. They could stay with her for a few weeks. Their grand-parents were anyway used to their being away from home at will, given their wild ways. No one would miss them anyway. As they gathered their bags for departure, Bablu realized he still had Jishnu's phone. "What do we do with this?", he asked Pappu, waving the mobile in his palms. Pappu looked at Bablu, "You might not like my suggestion". Bablu guessed Pappu's concern. "I don't want it, not this way", Bablu said softly. Pappu smiled. "Then let's throw it in the river downhill when we cross the bridge", he quipped.

~ * ~

Prabhu dropped the Mehta's at their home in East Delhi, the next evening. As soon as Jishnu was found and reunited with his parents, Namrata had made a big hue and cry about not wanting to stay in such an unsafe place. Their train reservations were for a later date, so Rishi hired Prabhu to drive them all the way back home, cutting short the holiday at Namrata's insistence. Rishi asked Prabhu to stop en-route at a temple to thank the almighty for Jishnu's wellbeing. Prabhu gladly obliged and made them pray at three! The trip to Delhi took them longer than required. They had to take a detour to avoid the wildfire that had spread on the way they would have normally taken. Rishi paid Prabhu his dues and tip and added an amount additionally. "In case you need something to sort out matters with the local police". Prabhu nodded in agreement.

~ * ~

"We need just a minute with the boy", the news reporter cajoled Namrata. "He has had enough attention and given enough interviews", Namrata replied coldly. "Maybe we could throw in your picture with him as well, please ma'am". So, for the nth time in the day, Jishnu repeated his story. How he saw a tall man trying to light up a fire near the resort, how he lost his balance and slipped, and how he was taken hostage. How he lost his mobile somewhere in the melee. How he was taken to a haunted house in the hills and how later he managed to escape when his abductor went out to get food. "Did he harm you, was he cruel", the reporter spurred him on, to gather as much as she could for what was to be her "breaking news" for the day. "No, on the contrary, he was nice, seemed he didn't really want to abduct me. He kept blabbering to himself about having to do such sins. I think he was poor", Jishnu enacted his well thought about story. "But you were missing for hours, why didn't the police come looking?", the reporter asked. "Well, they were stranded on their way because of a huge wildfire that surrounded the area, there was no other way they could have arrived", Nandita entered the camera frame, replying at her suave best. Jishnu ran away to his room, taking advantage of the situation. His gang of buddies was eagerly waiting there to hear more about his adventures in the haunted house.

~ * ~

A month later, Chandu met Pappu and Bablu in their village. He pulled out his mobile phone and showed them a video clip. "Thought this might interest you my friends", he said as the screen lit up. Pappu and Bablu saw Jishnu talking to a reporter about his escapade with his captive, a tall man who had still not been captured. He then went on a tirade about the responsibilities to protect the forests from these man-made wildfires. "Talks a lot, doesn't he? You guys had a lucky escape", Chandu smiled pausing the video and locking his phone. "By the way, now that you are back, unscathed, I had some work for you". Pappu and Bablu looked at each other and smiled. "Thanks, Chandu, but we have to rush for school!", Bablu replied and the two boys ran towards the village.

Chandu stood there puzzled for a while, then shrugged his shoulders, took out a pair of sunglasses, and flipped them over his face in style. "School? Again? Well…good for them, they can certainly do better", he spoke almost to himself before heading towards the road out of the village.

5

Purely Business

The ceiling fan creaked tiredly, unable to provide respite to the sweat building behind my ears. The summer heat invaded the room unabashedly through the open window, near which I was seated, mocking the fan's existence. The air conditioner in the room gathered dust despite the sweltering heat of Delhi.

I stared at Mr. Singh sitting on the dusty old sofa in front of me. He was wearing a full-sleeved white kurta as usual. His wrinkled hands trembled slightly as he brought the cup of green tea near his lips. His withered eyes lit up from behind the thick glasses that he wore, as he savoured the first sip of the tea, uncaring about his handsome white moustaches getting drenched in the beverage.

I shifted uneasily on the sofa opposite to him and glanced at my watch purposely to indicate a shortage of time.

"Mr. Singh, so when can I have the deposit back", I said, clearing my throat.

Mr. Singh, still mesmerized by the flavours of his green tea, slowly waved to me, indicating to lift my cup of the beverage. "Have it, Mr Vikas, it will get cold and lose its taste", he said softly, taking another sip followed by a sigh indicating a high sense of satisfaction.

I picked up the cup reluctantly and sipped on the tea. I couldn't understand what the fuss was about. Mrs. Singh had again boiled the water too long and dipped the tea bags for too short. The only saving grace was that there was no sugar in the beverage this time.

"Oh, you don't take sugar in your tea, is it?", Mr. Singh had asked me when we met a month back. "Not when I am having green tea or black tea", I had clarified. My reasoning, that the purpose of such brews as green tea was to keep fit, had gone down well with him.

"Malti ji", he had immediately turned back and called out to Mrs. Singh in the kitchen. "No more sugar in green tea from now on". I don't recall Mrs. Singh shouting back a confirmation, but believe I did hear the sound of a pan being thrown into the sink violently!

Unfortunately, my current meeting with Mr. Singh was going exactly like my last two meetings. Since the past twenty minutes or so he had deftly focused the conversation on myriad topics other than the refund of my security deposit which he held with him. It had been three months since I had vacated the apartment which I had rented from him five years ago, but I was yet to receive back the advance which I had paid to him as a refundable deposit while occupying the house. In my meetings and phone calls with him, he had been citing various reasons for the delay. Initially, he explained, he had invested that amount in a bank deposit and needed time to withdraw the money at a pertinent time to make some profits. "Each rupee counts for a retired old man with no real income, you see", he had quipped. In the second month, the excuse changed; "We are finalizing new tenants for the apartment. I will refund your money as soon as I receive a deposit from them". A few weeks later he expressed his anguish over not being able to find a suitable tenant. On my repeated pleas that I needed the money for getting some woodwork done for my new apartment, he yielded partially. Four green tea sessions later he handed me a cheque for half the amount! A month had gone by and I was now sitting in his house looking to recover the other half.

It was five years back that I had met Mr. Singh for the first time. I was searching for a bigger apartment to provide more personal space to each member of my family which had recently been expanded by the arrival of Anaya, our new-born daughter.

One of my neighbours introduced me to Mr. Singh who was looking to lease out an apartment he owned in an adjacent housing complex. I still remember that I had been offered green tea during my first interaction with Mr. Singh as well. I found him to be warm and cordial as a person on one side but very practical on the other. He took great interest in my job, family, and passions but was very straight about his demands on the financials of the deal. "Purely business, you see!" he had stated firmly when we first met at his residence.

In the years to follow I got to know more about him and his manners. He was a conformist, one who would always want rent cheques and any house-related notifications to be handed over personally to him, never believing too much in online transactions. He made sure he called me to his house on one pretext or another to discuss matters once a month. Since he lived only a block away, it never really bothered me. In fact, if I didn't show up, he used to show up at my residence unannounced at odd times, much to the chagrin of Vartika, my wife. So, she made sure that I paid Mr. Singh regular visits myself to avoid these surprises.

These meetings that were sold as quick catch-ups usually lasted for about an hour or sometimes even more. During this time Mr. Singh deftly allocated a mere ten minutes to my complaints related to the apartment like leakages and cracks in the wall or plumbing issues. Thereafter he conveniently steered (or so it seemed to me at that stage) the conversation to the state of affairs in the society, country, and the world at large for the rest of the time. Mrs. Singh who usually greeted me cheerfully when I arrived, preferred to stay away, appearing only once to complete the ritual of providing us our cup of green tea. Mr. Singh seemed to relish this part of the discussion and was always looking for more. I realized much later in life that I didn't probably mind those meetings much myself, as it gave me some free time away from the daily ordeals and more importantly provided a different perspective of life from an aged, experienced man.

The ceiling fan creaked some more, breaking the silence that otherwise filled the room.

Mr. Singh took the next sip. "So, how is your investment in the stock market going on?" he started one of his favourite threads of topics. "Not great, I do not get much time very frankly", I replied. "I know, people are so busy earning money these days that they don't have time for investing", he quipped. And for the next fifteen minutes, we spent time discussing the high and lows of the stock market, the trends, outlook, and in the end on how I should rejig my investment portfolio to earn some profits. He boasted of doing very well on some of his investments and I took that opportunity to bring back the topic to my deposit.

"So Mr. Singh, you were saying you will refund the remaining half of my deposit pending with you. I came for the cheque, am getting a bit late for office", I blurted. Mr. Singh looked at me gently, his expressions still unchanged. "Oh well, I did also say that the new tenant has still not arrived and he has to pay me that amount so that I could pay back to you!" he said, sighing. "But you just mentioned that you had earned a lot with your investments in stocks", I retorted, a bit shamelessly. "Oh, that! Well, I don't keep anything with me; I just transfer the profits to Malti Ji's account. You know I am getting old, just want to ensure, she has a good life after me. I keep all the accounts separate. Stock trade separate, housing account separate! Purely business, you know".

I knew he had played another trump card and I had lost the battle again. I felt no sense in dragging the meeting further. I could imagine my wife laughing aloud mockingly, "You couldn't do it this time as well. You are no naïve!"

As I was driving to work through the jammed roads of south Delhi, I pondered whether I really understood Mr. Singh after all these years. He appeared singularly stingy. I had always found him making excuses or delaying things when it came to matters involving expenditure. Whether it was the request for a fresh coat of paint to the house I lived in (and he owned) or putting grills on the windows to increase security, it was always dealt with casualness. But on the other side, he always took a keen interest in matters that required talking to or debating with people, be it housing society management, government officials, bank clerks, or even matters involving other residents of the building. Since he was happily retired for the last twenty years, he had enough time to invest in these discussions, and seldom often than not, he used to emerge victorious in them. It is debatable though whether it was his convincing skills or the sheer abundance of spare time that earned him those outcomes. However, his exploits made him undeservingly infamous with many who pretended to be helpful and caring for an old man up front but did not leave a stone unturned in joking about him behind his back. He continued unabated; perhaps unaware or perhaps simply not caring. I often felt that he just did it to keep himself busy. But on the other hand, I also felt he genuinely cared for the people around him. Having seen the world enough, he never shied away from giving some good elderly advice to all and sundry.

I still vividly remember an incident many years ago when I was sitting on the bench in a nearby park one day with Mr. Singh, discussing the unreasonable prices of real estate in the city. Mr. Singh halted our discussion abruptly and suddenly stopped a jogger completely unknown to us. The perplexed man did stop and it took a moment for both him and I to understand what was happening. Mr. Singh gently told the man that he had seen him watching going around the park multiple times and each time his feet had hit the drain cover that lay right in front of us in the middle of the jogging track. "You could easily go around it young fellow, you know how our infrastructure is crumbling these days, why take a risk!"

To his delight, the jogger felt humbled and sat down with us for a while as Mr. Singh went about introductions and ultimately making acquaintance.

When I reached back home that night, empty-handed as usual, Vartika asked sarcastically at the dinner table; "So, what's the date for the next meeting now?". I cringed. "Well, he has promised to get the cheque ready", I spoke softly, sounding unconvincing to even myself. "Oh really, how wonderful!" she smiled, looking at me. "Another week or two I suppose", she continued. "Yes", I blurted out, "Two weeks it seems". She continued to stare at me as if wondering whether she was drunk when she agreed to marry the man sitting in front of her.

"Dad, how is Moti?" Anaya asked lovingly, a twinkle in her eyes. I was glad someone spoke after the awkward silence. "Oh, he's good and healthy and playful as ever", I smiled back at her.

Anaya, now all of five, had seen Moti for the first time when he was still a pup. A mongrel, Mr. Singh had picked him up from the street one day when he was being chased by a pack of ferocious street dogs. Mr. Singh had brought him back to his residential compound with him, where he was kept near the reception for a few days. However, many residents started voicing concerns over the presence of a stray pup in the entrance lobby, and hence Moti, as Mr. Singh later christened him, was formally adopted to the Singh household. Moti proved to be a good company to the ageing Mr. Singh. He took him for long walks and chatted profusely with him. Perhaps Moti filled a void in his life.

When Anaya and I met them on one of these walks, both playful creatures gelled instantly. Mr. Singh was glad to see my daughter and invited her home, giving her a bait to have more fun time with the pup. For the next year or two, Anaya made sure she accompanied me on my evening walks at the time when she expected Mr. Singh and Moti to visit the neighbouring park. Mr. Singh always seemed delighted whenever he saw Anaya playing with Moti.

Time passed and as Mr. Singh's health deteriorated, he could no longer bring Moti down regularly. Moti and Anaya's meetings became less frequent. "Why don't you bring the little one along?", Mr. Singh had asked several times in our subsequent 'green tea' sessions. I intended to but somehow never could.

"Did you touch him, dad?" Anaya continued while sipping the soup placed in front of her. "Did he play with you?". "Well he did come to see me but since he realized that Anaya wasn't there, he went back"; I said tickling her. "Liar", she giggled, "I know he likes you too and so do you. He wouldn't have gone back!" she said playfully. I smiled. "Can I come along with you the next time dad? I miss him!".

As expected, I didn't hear back from Mr. Singh. Exactly at the end of two weeks, Vartika started babbling about my inability to get back even what was rightfully mine. It would be unfair to say that her jibes, which emanated with this particular case but soon encompassed my other unsuccessful exploits spanning a decade of our marriage, were the only reason for me to land up again at the Singh residence the following Sunday. Somewhere, I was losing patience as well and feeling cheated. Sensing my frustration or perhaps thinking I might become a wreck if I lose my temper, Vartika suggested taking Anaya along. Before I could delve into the merits of the suggestion Anaya was by my side wearing a bright pink frock, ready to leave.

As we walked from our building to Mr. Singh's, I was already silently rehearsing some impactful dialogues I had carefully prepared in case Mr. Singh made his lame excuses again. I had been kind enough and respected his age as much as I could. I needed to be tough this time, I told myself.

As I entered Mr Singh's apartment complex, Mahadev, the building's security guard, waved his hand. I knew Mahadev for long, not just because I met him each time I visited Mr. Singh, but also because he had earlier visited my last house umpteen times carrying written messages by Mr. Singh.

Mr. Singh didn't carry a smartphone. In fact, he barely used his old key phone as well. He sometimes used to call me over the landline, but since the line was usually bad, he fell back on his preferred method of writing notes.

His messages ranged from notes requesting bills that had barely arrived, to letters requesting me to drop him to different destinations on my way to the office. Mahadev, his usual messenger, sometimes even ferried small bottles filled with homeopathic medicines, which Mr. Singh sent for me. The accompanying notes would warmly say something like, "5 drops in the morning empty stomach to cure your headaches".

As I moved past Mahadev and got into the elevator, I wondered how Mr. Singh remembered everything I told him so vividly except monetary matters which specifically required outflows from his side!

"Say no to chocolates if aunty offers you any, remember?" I told Anaya as the weary-sounding elevator ascended slowly to its destination. She looked up and nodded in agreement. I could see a twinkle in her eye, in anticipation of meeting a long-lost friend.

Mrs. Singh opened the door and led us in after exchanging pleasantries. She went about her regular welcome routine of bringing us water to drink and some "Parle-G" biscuits. She offered them to Anaya, who looked at me before taking one of them. It was a few minutes later that Mr. Singh entered the room, looking more withered than before. He greeted me with his usual smile and his eyes lit up as soon as he saw the little one with me. "Look who's here, you have come after such a long time", he told her. Anaya smiled back, a little shy.

We settled ourselves in the dusty sofa, in the same orientation, as we always did, and started talking about the weather, as we always did. As we chatted, I could see Mr. Singh looking at Anaya's wondering eyes. "Malti Ji, can you unfasten Moti's leash. His friend has come!", he shouted out. "He's become very naughty, creates a lot of mess in the house which your aunty doesn't like, so we keep him tied for some hours", he told Anaya.

Moti came running into the room shortly and in an instant was jumping over Anaya. Excitement, giggling and woofing lit up the otherwise gloomy room for a few minutes. Mr. Singh and I sat quietly looking at Anaya and Moti's play. I could see a bright constant smile on Mr. Singh's otherwise shrunken face, as he watched the two make merry. Once Moti had his share of jumping around and settled down near my legs, I cleared my throat; "Mr. Singh I had come to take the cheque for the pending deposit". Mr. Singh sighed, "Some green tea Mr. Vikas?". As he turned back and called out, "Malti Ji…", I interrupted him. "No thanks Mr. Singh, I am in a hurry. Have to take Anaya to her dance class". "But today is Sunday dad, no classes!", Anaya quipped innocently. I glared at her. Mr. Singh caught the bluff and green tea arrived after some customary vehement clanking of utensils in the kitchen.

After ten more minutes of discussions on stock markets and the state of affairs in the nation, I brought up the purpose of my visit again. My usual temperate self was getting agitated, partly because of Mr. Singh's reluctance to cough up the money and partly because of my inability to make my anger visible to him. I could almost visualize my wife sitting on the sofa at home, on a call with her mother, complaining how unworthy I was.

Mr. Singh began with his usual grumblings and continued towards his elderly dependencies. Barring Anaya's presence in the room, it almost seemed to be a rerun of my last meeting with Mr. Singh. "I need the money, Mr Singh, my woodwork has been pending for the last few months because of that", I raised my voice, feeling both uneasy and silly. Mr. Singh seemed unperturbed. I wasn't sure whether I wasn't aggressive enough or he was prepared for it. A look at Anaya confirmed that I indeed spoke loudly. Mr. Singh launched into his 'purely business transaction' verbiage, explaining outflow couldn't happen without an inflow. I was flummoxed. I had no clue how to influence the old adamant man in front of me.

We reached home after an hour and a half. Rarely ever free otherwise, Vartika made sure she opened the door purposefully to look at my defeated face. She smiled wryly as I entered the house, her gaze never leaving me till I settled on the sofa. Anaya started babbling about the fun time she had with Moti but her mother wasn't interested in her escapades.

She came around and sat beside me, the wry smile still on her face. "So?" was her straight question. I stared at her for a while, then quietly pulled out a cheque from my pocket and handed it over to her. Her expression changed suddenly, almost as if someone reading a thriller realizes that the pages had been interchanged with a Paulo Coelho book. She also seemed perplexed that her knight in shining armour wasn't uttering any victory cries or thumping chests on this not so ordinary accomplishment!

And she was justified. The meeting with Mr. Singh was supposed to end, as expected, with another promise of making the funds available in another two weeks. After desperate attempts to put my case across, I was about to get up in frustration, when suddenly Mrs. Singh stormed into the room with a cheque in her hand.

She held out the cheque towards me and said softly, "Please take this, he had the cheque ready last week, but seems has forgotten about it". Mr. Singh seemed dumbstruck. He rose from the sofa and looked at her. "But the account doesn't have sufficient funds, Malti Ji...", but before he could finish Mrs. Singh cut him off with a stare. "I checked the balance yesterday and it's fine, why do you have to make him run again and again", she growled. She handed over the cheque to me and before I could say anything, she turned to Anaya and started talking with her.

I stood there looking at Mr. Singh who seemed a bit disappointed. "If it's a bother...", I started, not knowing what to say next. Mrs. Singh turned towards Mr. Singh and something silently exchanged between them. Mr. Singh smiled and settled again on his sofa. "Indeed, I might have had it ready, getting old you see", he was his usual self again. "So, then our records are settled", he said looking at me and then at Anaya playing with Moti. There was a strange forlorn look on his face as he looked at us. My return that day somehow seemed like a parting. Mr. Singh came down with us in the lift and walked with us for a while. "Keep visiting", he said when we finally shook hands.

And now, as Anaya prattled about the lovely time she had with Moti, I was in deep thought over what had transpired. I took the cheque back from Vartika and had a look. The amount seemed right. My eyes hovered above the cheque and found what they were looking for. The cheque was signed by Mrs. Singh. It was a joint account and the co-holder had asserted her right. This even puzzled me more and somehow, I don't know why, I felt sad.

The cheque was deposited, the amount credited and consumed (not on the woodwork, as had been my winning pitch, but instead for flight tickets for a leisure trip). Days passed by and then months. The stock markets rallied and tumbled and rallied again. The weather took its course. Anaya started liking green tea, rather rare for her age and I got busier at work and a lot more aloof from my friends and family. Vartika, well she remained as ever, nothing changed for her.

Almost a year later, I received a call while on my way to the office. It was Mrs. Singh. She spoke softly, "Mr. Vikas, do you remember me?". "Of course, I do, aunty", I replied promptly. "How's Mr. Singh?", I asked. The response came after a pause of a few seconds, "He breathed his last two weeks ago". "Oh, I am sorry, I did not know else I would have come!", was all I could manage. "It's alright; do you mind coming over today or tomorrow for a while?"

Mahadev greeted me as I entered Mr. Singh's housing complex that evening. He informed me that Mr. Singh wasn't keeping well since the last month, had been in and out of the hospital multiple times. His son, who lived in Australia, could never manage to arrive in time.

Mrs. Singh looked the same though. The pain and angst that one would expect to find on one's face in such a situation were missing. Instead, there was a stoic calm, which I respected.

She offered to make some green tea and smiled. I smiled back, nodding my head, refusing. She got up and went inside, and as I was waiting, Moti came running and sat by me gladly. I patted and played with him, waiting for Mrs. Singh to return. When she did, she had an envelope in her hands. "He knew he was not going to survive long when he came back from the hospital last month. Wrote many letters and notes one day and explained to me what to give to whom. This one is for you", she informed, handing me the sealed envelope.

"Dear Mr. Vikas,

It was wonderful knowing you all these years. I am not keeping too well these days so taking this time to clear some of life's dues. I am sorry for keeping you waiting for so many days to return your deposit. I believed in keeping each transaction separate as I stated to you, even though I had the balance in my other accounts. However, when I was on the hospital bed, I realized that it was unfair to you. It was selfish to call you time and again. I am not sure whether it was my reluctance to part with the money or the joy of spending time with you. I immensely enjoyed our intellectually stimulating discussions over tea. It's rare to find reasonable people like you these days.

Enclosed with this letter you will find a cheque, please accept it as a small gift from my side for your daughter. I know you are a self-made man so if you find it difficult to accept it that way think of it as an interest on the money that I owed to you all these months.

Purely business transaction, you see!"

At the end of the letter was a note in a more fumbled handwriting and different coloured ink as if written a few days later;

P.S.- You can now add Bryonia Alba to the last medicine I suggested for your headache. You can get it at the chemist near our building. "

"He felt a certain calm after writing all these letters"; Mrs. Singh said softly. "He just had one worry", she said softly looking at Moti who had snuggled near my feet.

A few days later Vartika stood wide-eyed yet silent in the living room staring at the pandemonium in front of her. Moti had just flipped her slippers into the air and was running wildly from one room to the other, happily exploring his new abode. Anaya and I were running after him trying to grab his leash, things falling and crashing all around. A glance at Vartika's face and I knew that she was already wondering whether her decision, to allow the dog to be a part of our family, had indeed been wise.

"It's going to be alright!", is all I could muster to say to her, as she walked out of the house, dialling her mother's number on her phone.

6

THE DREAM

Her mother once told her, dreams that you have early in the morning, and remember, come true.

Jenny woke up suddenly, early in the morning, and remembered having a horrific dream. She sat in her bed, trembling, and feeling cold. She glanced at the clock. It was barely five and the sun had not yet come up. She felt stifled and choked and decided to have a bath. She shrugged off the bad memories from the morning as she got ready for her dance classes.

Jahanvi Mehra or Jenny, as she liked to be called, was a peppy nineteen-year-old, having a passion for dance that surpassed any other feeling known to her. She was obsessed with her dance practice sessions and was proud to be good at them. She mixed her hobby and her studies at the college with aplomb to the delight of her parents and teachers.

She reached her dance class early that day. The hall was empty. She was about to start rehearsing her steps when she heard footsteps behind her. She turned around to find a tall, thin girl standing at the entrance. She was a newcomer to their troupe. Since there was still some time before everyone came in, the two girls started introductions and were soon indulged in chatting profusely about their common passion.

~

In her dream, Jenny had seen a flurry of bewildering images and sequences. Images that made no sense. Things that could not be. Things that she had no connection with. She saw them in interrupted flashes with no relation between them. Most of the time, she didn't remember what she dreamt but this time she did, every tiny bit of it.

Dreams know no rules, they defy everything. Logic, reason, nothing holds. They are so different from the real world and yet so near. In her dream, Jenny remembered coming by a very old friend, a friend whom she had been away for years. She remembered how glad she felt when they sat together and made up for the lost time. Next, she dreamt that she was sitting in a friend's house and her friend introduced her to a handsome charming young man, whose face she barely remembered. She remembered her friend pointing out that the suave man was her brother. She remembered the elation when the gentleman flirted and wooed her with all his charms. She also dreamt of something absolutely weird. She saw a white cat with long whiskers moving round and round in circles. She remembered her confusion at the strange feat being performed by the cat. She hated cats and tried to shoo her away but the cat just looked at her and meowed and went back doing her rounds.

~

Jenny's friendship with Tina, the new girl in the dance troupe developed quite fast. They both seemed to be having similar tastes and this cemented their bond. Tina called Jenny home one day. While Tina was busy making coffee, Jenny wandered about the living room, looking at Tina's childhood photographs. Her attention was caught by a black and white photograph that seemed familiar. It was a school photograph with lots of children standing in rows, proudly sporting their school uniforms. Jenny stared at the photograph in bewilderment. Tina returned with the coffee and observing Jenny staring at the photograph, she remarked, "Oh, that's an old one. When I was in class three. Had great fun at school, hardly remember anyone now though!". Jenny's hands trembled. She had a copy of the photograph herself at home!

When it turned out that Tina and Jenny were once childhood classmates, Tina was elated. But Jenny was vexed. It had merely been a week since she saw the dream and she remembered it vividly still. She couldn't help but relate her meeting Tina to the dream that she saw. Her joy easily gave way to confusion and confusion to fear. She had a reason to feel that way. Apart from the reunion with her friend, the encounter with her friend's brother, their subsequent courtship, and the furry white cat doing strange antics, there was one more thing she remembered from her dream. And the very thought of it sent shivers through her.

~

In the dream that Jenny saw, her friends' brother grew intimate with her. They had a strong relationship going. In one of the flashes, she remembered dreaming about them sitting in a boat on placid waters. He was holding her hand and saying something. She on the other hand was listening to the splash of the boat in the water. Suddenly she saw him get up and push her firmly and intentionally out of the boat and into the water.

She still remembered the stifling feeling she had as she dreamt of drowning. That was when she had woken up suddenly. That was how the dream had ended.

Jenny tried to dismiss her reunion with Tina and its proximity to the dream as mere coincidence. However, somewhere in the back of her mind, the thought stayed, perhaps because of the end. She once asked Tina, "Do you have any brothers?". "No", Tina had replied. "Do you like cats?" she had asked another time. "I hate them, just like you", Tina shot back. Jenny felt better.

~

 Tina got engaged to a doctor a few days later. She had an affair going on with him for a long time. Jenny was invited to the engagement party. Tina had specifically instructed her to keep her eyes open for all the eligible bachelors. Jenny didn't like parties much and Tina's engagement party was no different. She felt completely out of place in the surrounding revelry and glitz. She decided to leave early. She looked around for Tina to bid her farewell, but couldn't find her. She lingered there for another half an hour and then her patience ran away. She stepped out of the house and started walking towards her car. "Jenny", came an unfamiliar voice from behind. A smartly dressed young man was walking up to her. "Excuse me, do I know you?" she inquired. "No, you don't, but I do. You're the woman I am destined to be with, according to Tina". He shrugged his shoulders and smiled cunningly. Jenny was confused. "Umm… that's till the time we get to Evergreen Sweets and back". He smiled again, explaining. "You see Tina seems to have run out of sweets and wants you to guide me to the shop as I am new to the area". He flashed his smile again and pointed backwards. Tina stood at the door to her house. She waved to Jenny and shouted, "Hurry up you two". The young man smiled as he saw Jenny grasping what had to be done.

"Ok, let's go"; she said. "Your car or my Mercedes?" he asked grinning. She smiled "Your Mercedes".

~

The Mercedes turned out to be a neat Honda. The young man introduced himself as Raj. Jenny noted that he was a gregarious man and garrulous too. She had never known anyone up close with such a gift of the gab. When she asked him how he knew Tina, he replied, "Well, I am her finance's neighbours' son". By the time they got back from the shop, they were friends.

Raj was a magnet. He attracted Jenny as no one did. From the day she first met him, Jenny knew that he was very special. Raj was also unashamed in showing his interest in their relationship and showering all his attention on her. They started meeting regularly and a very strong bond developed between them. Months passed by and their relationship bloomed but still remained oblivious to Tina. On the day of Tina's marriage, a month later, Raj and Jenny went up to her together to congratulate her, smiling naughtily at each other. Tina started introducing them to her other friends. Jenny was introduced and then it was Raj's turn. Tina told her friends "And this is Raj, my cousin". "But he told us he's your fiancé's neighbour's son", someone remarked. "I know", Tina smiled wryly at Raj. "That's how this smarty likes to introduce himself. It's true though, he's my husband's friend. He lives adjacent to my husbands' house. See the connection? I met my husband thanks to him!". Jenny went blank.

~

After Tina's wedding, Jenny tried to avoid Raj, as the memories of her nightmare still haunted her.

The reunion with an old friend, Jenny getting close to her brother, if only a cousin, surely it couldn't all have been a coincidence. However, the more she avoided Raj, the more they bumped into each other. At parties, in the market, at the disco, almost everywhere she went. Raj constantly tried to contact Jenny but she would not take his calls and ignore him when they crossed somewhere. Around a month later, she bumped into him again and he coerced her into a talk. He inquired what was wrong with her and why she was avoiding him. Jenny yielded this time and they sat together for coffee, Raj doing most of the talking. Raj said he could sense something wrong and suggested they go somewhere for a change. He proposed to visit the nearby island caves. Jenny found the request strange. She knew that meant taking a boat ride to the island. Knowing Raj's dislike for sea rides she was confused. She sneered "Why? You're not interested in sea rides, so why this now". "Because you like it, it's your kind of thing, these artistic caves. I'll have fun if it's with you, never mind my seasickness. We will hire a personal boat". Jenny was aghast. She had just been presented a proposal to be in a boat with Raj. Was her dream coming true? She got up saying a rude no and left for her house.

~

The next day however Jenny was overwhelmed by the situation. Why would Raj want to drown her, they were good friends, well actually lovers, or so she believed. She had daydreamed about spending her life with him many times, so did this silly notion that she nestled make any sense? Jenny saw no reason, but then could all that was happening be merely a coincidence, all the events that she witnessed merely luck? Maybe she didn't remember all the details of the dream, maybe she just didn't see it or maybe it was just a reflection of her conscience. But Jenny knew she couldn't fool herself. She very well remembered what she had dreamt and understood that she would be never able to forget it until she tried to avoid it.

This cannot go on like this forever, she thought. She had to get this raging tumour out of her head. Let the dream become a reality or let it perish once and for all. If she could believe such wild theories, she should also believe that whatever was destined to happen, will happen, no matter what. She reasoned that since she knew the outcome, she could perhaps change it, in case the worst happened. She made up her mind, picked up the phone, and called Raj.

~

Raj and Jenny sat together, all alone in the ferry's lower deck seating area, a good ten miles away from the shore. There were only two other people on the boat apart from them, the motorman and an assistant who were confined to their cabins, chattering as they sped towards the island housing the caves. The lower deck was air-conditioned and closed from all sides with dark mirrors. Raj had made sure all the curtains were drawn to ensure privacy. Jenny realized that Raj would have had to plan this since the interiors of the boat were cleaned and well-arranged which she had never found when she had travelled by such boats in groups. To her surprise, Jenny did not find Raj being any wee bit uncomfortable, as she would expect of a person having seasickness. She remembered Raj having told her about some of his boat trips at sea which had turned horrid for him. But today he sat there almost with a quirky smile on his face.

There was a knock on the door to the area they sat in and the assistant walked in with an icebox, the neck of a bottle of wine gleaming out of it. Jenny felt the assistant's gaze on her from the corner of his eyes and a hint of a smirk on his face. As he moved out Raj handed him a note and locked the door from within. Jenny was getting nervous and was now thinking it wasn't probably a good idea to have come here. She was confused about the entire setup. They barely spoke. Jenny waited for Raj to make a move. When nothing happened, unable to bear the tension anymore, she got up suddenly to get out for some fresh air. Raj got up as well and in a swift motion grasped her from the back. He held her tight and started kissing her profusely, his hands wavering over Jenny's body. Jenny was horrified; she couldn't understand what was going on. She smelled alcohol on Raj, but the wine lay unopened yet. She cried, "Raj, stop it!" and pulled out of his hands as he relaxed his grip. "Are you mad?" she yelled as she walked out fuming and climbed the stairs to the upper open deck of the boat. Raj rushed out after her and cried aloud in the wind "Jenny, what is this, get back here". Raj climbed up the stairs to the upper deck, "Please get back here, the sea's rough. The motorman says it's not safe up there". Jenny was too enraged to yield to logic. She continued to yell "What were you trying to do? And you're drunk?". "Jenny I am not drunk, this is some toddy concoction the motorman gave me for seasickness that is smelling. It worked for a while but is now doing more harm than good I think". Raj tried to reason, moving towards her slowly while trying to balance himself. "And I am sorry I just wanted to kiss, I wanted to show you something". The shrieking wind in Jenny's ears made it difficult for her to hear or understand much. She got closer to the edge of the boat, just a small railing between her and the green foaming sea.

She sensed Raj approach from behind and turned around to face him to ask the question which nagged her. Why? As she turned, a huge wave hit the boat, rocking it sideways, throwing Jenny off balance, over the rail, and into the sea.

~

She woke up in the hospital, hours later. She learnt from her mother how the boatmen saved her. She enquired about Raj and came to know that he was also recuperating in the adjacent room. He was the first one to have thrown himself into the water before the boatman jumped in. He had clung to her to keep her safe before the boatmen could pull them in. Jenny could only mutter; "But how's that possible, he doesn't... he doesn't know how to swim!". His mother just nodded in agreement.

A few days later Raj sat next to her. Tears rolled down Jenny's eyes, "Why did you do it?". "Had to learn swimming someday. No better way to start, I thought", he flashed the same smile that had lit up Jenny's world ever since he entered her life. Raj looked at her and got serious. "Couldn't think of losing you", he said as he pulled out a ring from his pocket. "This is what I wanted to show you that day, it was in the icebox that was brought in on the boat. Would you marry me?" he asked earnestly. She nodded happily, tears rolling down her cheeks. They hugged and she asked; "Anything else?". He looked up and said naughtily; "Yes, I know you hate them, but can we keep a cat?". Jenny laughed, as she had never done earlier in her life. She felt silly to have let a dream rule her life for so long. She decided to embrace the happiness that was coming her way with both her arms.

"Guess I should take time out to learn swimming too if we have to do that trip again", she smiled.

~

They got married that winter. Love prospered and they made a cosy couple, snatching attention wherever they went. Jenny resumed her dance classes a month after her marriage. Raj grew up the ladder in his advertising firm. They kept a white cat. The dream was laughed out of Jenny's life.

Time flew as it always does. Jenny worked hard on grooming and blossoming her talent. She had her first stage performance two years after their marriage. Raj got a special seat in the first row and was mentioned in her speech of thanks. She became a star overnight. She signed many contracts for shows in India and on foreign lands.

More work meant a more hectic schedule, Jenny became very busy. In her spare time at home, she and Raj shared their lives and cooked together. She taught her white cat to do rounds as if mocking the dream which had changed her life. They both laughed and giggled as the little creature tripped and fumbled in learning the trick.

As both grew in their careers, Jenny rather rapidly, they bought a villa outside the metropolis, with an organic farm to boast of. The villa overlooked a beautiful lake and was surrounded by low mountains. It satiated their need to break free from their busy lives and return to tranquillity on weekends to be with themselves.

Jenny started doing films. Her superlative dancing skills enhanced her appeal to the audience and she found herself touching the zenith of her career. As she became more famous,

Jenny became a media favourite. They wrote about her lifestyle, her mannerism even her eccentricities. They flashed her likes and dislikes. When this got stale, they wrote about her differences with Raj. They reported about another woman in his life. Jenny grew in stature and popularity by the day. Raj stagnated in his career in the advertising firm. Jenny's schedule took over her life. They spent lesser and lesser time with each other. Time flew by and Jenny and Raj drifted apart.

~

Ten years after she had the nightmare, Jenny was found dead. Her body was fished out from the lake nearby her residence. She had been reported missing for a week. The media smelt blood. They suggested she had been drowned on purpose. The media buzzed with reports citing various reasons for the probable murder. Raj was questioned but the police didn't get any substantial evidence or confirmed theories. The post mortem declared death by drowning with no other signs of physical injuries. Raj was constantly spotted with an attractive woman a few months after Jenny's death.

~

When the investigating team reached Jenny's house a month after her death, they were greeted by a white cat with big whiskers. In the lush green lawns in front of the house, the investigations team stood in admiration watching the feline beauty meow and go about doing something they had never seen a cat do before: go round and round in perfect circles.

Bringing Up Ted

Sid and Ollie first made preliminary rounds in and around the house. They then settled for a spot between the two walls on the patio. Frankly speaking, I wasn't impressed much by their choice. Not because they had chosen to make a nest within the confines of our house but because the spot that they had chosen was too small for the purpose. I tried to make them change their mind by shooing them away now and then but they stuck to their choice and before I could do anything else, their nest was ready.

I had been watching these two grey pigeons fly and roam around my house for quite a while, cooing mellifluously and assessing the house with idiosyncratic jerks of their small heads. Sid, who I later inferred to be the male, had more stripes and spots than Ollie who was predominantly grey. Once they had decided the location for the nest Sid and Ollie got busy with collecting twigs and straws and bringing them to the spot chosen by them. Their visits to my house, therefore, became very frequent. This in turn led my pet dog Tobu to develop a strong dislike for them. He barked and roared and chased them in and around the house whenever he could. But Sid and

Ollie were brave creatures and in a few days' time Ollie was cosily sitting in her small nest as Sid watched from afar.

Ollie laid eggs and before I knew it Ted and Harry had said hello to the world. Since their nest was at a good height, my first view of Ted and Harry came when they had grown a few days old. I climbed a portable ladder one day, to replace a faulty light bulb in the patio, and visible from above was the little haven of Ted and Harry, small bundles of ruffled grey feathers, bobbing up and down in the nest. Ollie, behaving like a responsible mother, kept close to them keeping a strict vigil. With the three of them precariously perched on the top in that insufficient and inappropriate space, I could only hope that Ted and Harry behaved themselves well.

Sid meanwhile kept watch from a distance but was frequently out on business trips. He didn't go anywhere near the nest but assisted Ollie in collecting food for the kids whenever Ollie came out of the nest. Ollie on the other hand had a lot to do at home. Feeding the young ones, keeping guard, and grooming them was all her responsibility. I could see her going about her chores from my room but to get a view of the newly born twosome I had to use the ladder. Even then I couldn't get close enough and longed to see Ted and Harry from near. My wish was granted soon but, in a manner, I would have never wanted it to be.

As soon as Tobu was let out on the lawn early the next morning, he started barking furiously. I went outside to ascertain the cause and found Tobu on the porch, staring at Harry, who had fallen from the nest and lay on the floor, motionless and still. Harry's death only confirmed my belief that the spot at which the nest was built was not fit for the purpose. I knew something had to be done to prevent Ted from meeting the same fate. That afternoon, while Ollie was out to get food, I arranged for my ladder to reach out to a spot just beneath the nest. A stinking smell emanated from the nest. Ted lay snuggled in the nest occasionally fluttering his feathers, I took my first good look at the nest and the problem was evident. The area was certainly much lesser than that required for a family of three. The problem was compounded by the downward sloping surface on which the nest lay. One unlucky move by Ollie or Ted and the whole nest and its occupants would surely fall all the fifteen feet to the ground.

I tried to provide a safety wall to the nest by fixing a small piece of ply at the entrance but the nails required to hold it would just not drive in the hard-cemented pillar. I tried a few other similar measures but nothing worked out. Meanwhile, Ollie was back and fluttering around the nest anxiously doubting my motives. Defeated and out of ideas, I climbed down the ladder.

Ted fell from the nest the same day but survived the fall. I found him lying in the verandah, surrounded by his droppings, in the evening. I bent down to have a closer look at him. He was nothing more than a mass of stinking grey feathers. His eyes, tiny black buttons in the small round head that was jetting out from the rest of the body, were half shut and he breathed heavily. I was confused about what my next move should be. Harry's death loomed before my eyes and I knew Ted's chances of surviving the fall were poor. Still, I knew I had to do my bit for him. I brought a large plastic dustbin lid and covered the surface with all the twigs and dry leaves that I could find. I brought the makeshift nest near Ted who was oblivious of me and my brother standing above him, maybe due to the damage done by the fall, physically or mentally. I was almost afraid to pick him up in my hands lest I touch some wounded part and hurt him. So I brought a piece of cardboard and gently nudged him in with it. He squeaked slowly and twirled a few times but finally settled down in his new home. I then kept him under the shade of a plant in my garden and bade him goodnight. That night I pondered quite a while about how to save Ted's life and take care of him. Suddenly a part of Sid and Ollie's responsibilities had been handed over to me and I had no idea how to cope with it.

The next morning when I woke up, I found my younger brother muttering something. I strained my eyes and ears and heard him telling me something about Ted. "He's back in his actual nest", he reported, "What? How?", I enquired, puzzled and fully awake now.

"The gardener came today morning on his weekly trip and put Ted back in the nest. He said it was best for him if his mother looked after him. I also thought it was the best decision to make", continued my brother. "He anyway wasn't eating anything by himself when we gave him some small pieces of food". I rushed out and glanced up at the nest. Ollie was visible in the nest, dipping her head regularly apparently to feed or groom Ted. I returned to my room. "What do you say?" asked my brother. "The gardener is a fool. I tell you the spot of the nest itself is not right. What if he falls again?", was all I could manage.

I kept an eye on the nest throughout the day. I even climbed up the ladder a couple of times to check Ted's position in the nest. He seemed to be doing fine and looked happy in Ollie's company. I started working on a plan to surround the nest with protective wiring.

A day went by. My plans were not ready but things seemed to be going fine. I was beginning to believe that the gardener had indeed done the right thing by putting Ted back in the nest when Ted fell again. This time it was my father who spotted him lying on nearly the same spot as earlier. Somehow Ted miraculously survived the second fall too. There were more droppings and the same stinking smell around him, and as before he breathed heavily. But the mass of feathers was moving a bit this time. I brought his makeshift home near him and once again nudged him in. This time I did it with my hands and touching Ted seemed wonderful.

But the question was, could Ted survive the second fall especially since they had occurred in such succession. I had no earlier experience with bringing up birds and my reasoning told me that it was very difficult for Ted to make it. After all little Harry had not even survived the first fall, how could Ted survive two?

I woke up early the next morning and rushed to the lawn. Ted lay all puffed up, showing no signs of movement. I strained my eyes as I got closer, and to my relief I found him breathing. Ollie and Sid were nowhere to be seen. The question that constantly hovered in my mind was how to feed this tiny bundle of feathers that lay motionless in front of me. And what? I presumed that something semi-solid would do the trick and so I put some boiled, mashed rice in front of Ted. Somewhere in my heart, I knew I was being too optimistic. I knew Ted wouldn't be able to eat anything orally so soon.

After all, just a day before Ollie was forcing something down his throat using her beak. To add to my woe, he wouldn't even open his eyes and sense the food. Now and then he fluttered his semi-formed wings and then again went into hibernation.

Thankfully this didn't last long. Ollie found the new nest in the garden in the afternoon that day and brought him food. Nature had its way and Ted his meal. The only problem now seemed to be was the proper placement of Ted's new home. Since it was very different from what Ollie had built fifteen feet up, Ollie only came to feed and groom her baby. At other times Ted lay all alone in the garden. We had to move his makeshift nest here and there to avoid him being exposed to the harsh summer sun. Ted, it seemed clearly enjoyed the change in scenery for his small head frantically bobbed up and down, right, and left as soon as we shifted him from one spot to another.

My dog Tobu was rather puzzled by this new creature on which everybody was showering so much attention but chose to remain neutral. He continued to frighten away Sid and Ollie but chose to ignore Ted. In fact, in response to our concern, he went up to Ted's nest now and then to sniff and check if everything was all right.

A day went by and then another. Ted seemed to be normal; he had emerged unscathed from those two falls. He was now growing and that ugly mass of feathers was gently taking shape. To be precise he was now starting to look like a bird. All these days when Ted lay in the open, day and night, we never thought of Kitty. It just didn't cross my mind before one night, when I was checking on Ted, covering him with a small piece of cloth to prevent him from the dew, that I heard Kitty meow.

I looked up and saw her on the rooftop, her eyes glowing in the dark. A sudden shudder ran through me. What if Kitty had seen Ted? The cat would be thinking of a feast. And I cursed myself for not thinking of this before. Kitty stayed away from the house because of Tobu. But I couldn't take chances since my dog stayed indoors during the night. It was then that I decided to keep Ted inside the safety of my house for the nights. I couldn't let Kitty meet Ted. Contrary to my belief though, Kitty didn't play the villain, not even during the daytime when Ted lay alone in the garden enjoying the greenery around. And that about ends the role of Kitty in the story.

Ted grew faster than our expectations and became a sheer delight to watch. Sid and Ollie dutifully dispensed their parental duties day in and day out. Ted now began to recognize me and my brother and now allowed us to get near him without getting anxious. It seemed we were no longer a bunch of strange monsters to be afraid of.

One afternoon, more than three weeks half after his second fall, Ted realized he had wings and that he could use them. It was a bright afternoon when Ted seeing me approach started flapping his wings furiously. This time his wings answered his call and carried him into the air. He rose a foot from the ground and then fell sharply. My heart sank for a moment. But diehard as he was, he repeated the act, went a few more feet in the air, and crashed into a small plant in the garden. I waited for him to try again. He did not fly but stared at me with questioning eyes as if to say, "Guess that's enough for today!". And so, I had to bring his mobile nest near him for him to get in. He didn't seem to be in a mood to oblige and rather preferred his day out. So, I let him be. He was back in his seat in the evening taking a rest after the day's endeavours. Ted continued to toss up and down utilizing the newfound strength in his wings for the next couple of days. His stints soon became patterns and patterns turned into flight. We could now see the little bird fly from his nest to the nearby plants and back.

"Hey, wake up"; implored my brother. "Ted's sitting on the neighbour's boundary wall". Blinking my eyes and still confused, I rushed to the scene. Ted, our small little champion, was eying my neighbour's garden from our boundary wall. "He wants to go places now!" I smiled. "He'll leave us anytime now". I ignored my younger brother's plea to bring him back to his nest. "Let him be. It's time he goes out into the real world!", I muttered sadly.

Ted returned to our garden in a few hours. He however abandoned his nest permanently. He preferred being perched on the branches of the plants and trees around. Strangely Sid and Ollie were nowhere to be seen to see their young one fly. Maybe they had already realized earlier what I came to know that day. Ted was ready to explore the world.

Ted went missing in the afternoon. We waited for hours, searched every nook and corner of the house, but he was nowhere to be seen. We knew it was all over. Ted had embarked on his journey to measure the skies. However, Ted chose to prolong the farewell by returning to the boundary wall in the evening. He was taking some serious lessons in flying. And he now looked smarter and more confident.

The next day however nothing similar happened. As we watched him practicing his manoeuvres sipping our tea, Ted suddenly flew a long way, paused for a few seconds on the metallic gate to our house, glanced back, and then bade us goodbye forever.

A month or so later after Ted left, another pigeon couple started planning a nest at the same spot that Sid and Ollie had chosen. Since I knew the choice was wrong, I shooed them away several times. But adamant as they are, the pigeons returned every time.

This time, however, I was adamant too. I brought out the ladder one fine day and blocked the space by cementing it with a plank of wood. I did so not because I didn't want to see another Ted grow up in front of me, only to fly away one day. I did so because I did not want another Harry to have a fatal fall and miss the opportunity to fly free in the blue skies like his brother Ted.

8

TOGETHER FOREVER

"Then victorious we shall be,
With everything set right,
We'll be extolled by all,
With all pride,
That day will come, love,
It will…"

The poet put down his pen and gazed out of the window. The lifeless mountains, that loomed over the few scattered houses around, stood silently in the early morning mist . The sun was beginning to spread its radiance across the sky. Life was creeping back in the small town after the long and dark night. "Now where the hell are you? ", came an angry voice from inside the house. The poet closed his eyes and took a deep breath. His day had begun.

"You don't do any work all day, do you?", his wife nagged. "Ever thought about home? Seems you've sworn not to take notice of me and this house. Your pen is what you love and nothing else"; she shouted from the neighbouring room. "There are no vegetables in the house for today!", she continued at the top of her voice as she entered his room, moving around briskly, dusting the furniture. "I remember I brought some yesterday, what happened to…", the poet started but was cut short in between. "Well, I had a grand feast yesterday all for myself when you had gone out to meet your stupid publisher friend", she scorned, giving him a cruel look.

The poet walked out of the room without further argument. He let himself down on the grass in his small garden, outside the house, and remembered the woman he had married. She had transformed completely over these years and he never knew why.

"What do you want, after all, it's my work. That's what I do best", he said gulping morsels of his lunch hurriedly, to avoid the latest confrontation of the day. "Scribbling throughout the day, building up fantasies about people and places that do not exist, preaching sermons in your articles when you can't even control your own house, that's what you call work? Get real, you have tried enough, it's high time to go out and get engaged in some other work", his wife replied almost trembling with rage. "What have I ever done, for God's sake, to deserve these harsh looks? I am trying", he said, choking, almost on verge of tears.

He was a gifted poet and writer, feelings flowed out spontaneously from his pen and spilled themselves into heart-wrenching words on paper. He had majored in arts in college and took to writing while he was still studying. He realized that he could convey the thoughts and turbulence in his mind better by writing than by debating. He was adjudged the best writer innumerous times in college and local functions. But once out from the college in a small town, he realized that there was a big competitive world out there that had its dynamics. He tried his luck at various newspapers in small and big cities but his contributions were almost always confined to the insignificant pages and badly manipulated by the publishers. Some run-of-the-mill writing assignments did come his way but he realized soon that it was not his forte to write on someone else's instructions. He found his independent writings to be more fulfilling. He didn't want his works to be manipulated. Some critics had forecasted a great future for him, seeing his work, but despite all such recommendations he had not found success in getting even one independent work released by a major publisher.

He was in a financial mess after few years of his marriage due to this. He had told his wife about his passions and his financial conditions before their marriage, but they had loved each other then and she gladly made an alliance with the circumstances. They decided to move to this small town in the hills to cut expenses and live an easier life. They planned to create their small haven here, despite all limitations. But as years went by something somewhere went wrong. The woman he loved changed dramatically, he never could get certain why. Perhaps because of the hardships, perhaps because of the kind of work that he did, perhaps missing family, perhaps children which she said they couldn't afford to have. The paradise that he dreamt of building had ended up being an inferno for them. And his poems, which she so loved back in her college days had become insignificant to her.

Distraught from all quarters, he had recently pursued the lone publisher in the town to publish his work at the poet's own cost. This had made his financial condition worst and had been the final nail in the coffin. His wife abhorred the decision and they barely talked sense after that incident.

"Where are you dear", her voice went ringing through the rooms of the silent bungalow. She had never sounded this delighted in years. "The news just came in, seems your publisher friend had forwarded your collection to the National Literary Counsel without your knowledge, and guess what, you have won a national award!". "Where are you?", she said entering the house from the garden and hurtling herself towards his room. "I cannot tell you how excited I am. You should've seen everyone's expression in the streets when I broke the news", she exclaimed removing the curtains that covered the entrance to his room.

She glanced around and found him resting head down on his study table. The papers around were drenched in red with the blood that trickled from his wrist. She opened her mouth to cry, but her voice failed her as if mocking her. The curtains on the window in the room gave way to the strong breeze that pushed itself inside and tossed up the papers on the table. A few of them dropped instantly, heavy with the blood on them, a few which were not touched, flew across the room. One of them rose high and landed on her feet. She picked up the paper, her fingers getting smeared with the traces of blood that was present on the sheet.

It read:

"When we shall both smile again,
When the world will know it's true,
When you shall be proud of me,
And I shall be of you,
That day will come, love,
It will ..."

9

CHANDANI

It had been a long time since we came across any signs of civilization. So, it was a natural reaction to start staring at whatever establishments, houses, or shops that passed by us as our taxi crossed a village. The road narrowed as we entered the village. Playful children crowded both sides of the street, some playing with pebbles, others spinning cycle tyres around with sticks. The older ones engaged themselves in street cricket, using the road as their pitch, running to the sides as a vehicle passed by, and resuming their play as soon as it crossed them.

"Be careful and drive slow, Yadav ji", I told the driver who nodded in agreement. I looked out of the window again and found few women, sitting outside the houses on the roadside, braiding each other's hair. Few others could be seen busy cutting raw mangoes to be used later for pickles. Just where the village ended, there loomed a small hillock. Apart from a few scanty trees here and there, it looked mostly barren, the scorching sun snatching away all the greenery it would have gathered during the monsoons. On the top of the mountain, I could see a small temple with a saffron flag fluttering gallantly on top of it.

"Let's stop here somewhere and have tea", I suggested to my friend who accompanied me. He seemed delighted by the idea.

We were en-route to a friend's marriage in Nagpur. We had hired a taxi from Mumbai, unable to get any train reservations due to our dilly-dallying on the plan. It turned out to be a great decision as we hit the road, leaving behind the madness of the city, and having fresh breeze hit our face to rejuvenate the soul. It had been a comfortable journey so far. We asked our way to a small tea stall, a little down the main road. The owner asked our pardon for not having an arrangement to sit. We were more than happy to stand and stretch ourselves after the long ride on the cosy seats of the Indica. As tea was being prepared, my friend went looking for a place to relieve himself, and I walked towards the rear of the small shop. There in its full view was the hillock that had caught my attention. The temple on it was visible much clearer from here. I zoomed in on the temple using the powerful lens on my camera and took a few pictures. The wind blew in my ears and with it brought the faint but unique sound of temple bell ringing in the distance. The entire scenario was very soothing and peaceful and aroused a strange interest within me.

I walked back to the tea stall owner. "What's the temple there at the top of the hill, is it visited by the village folk?" I enquired. "Yes sir, it's the most sacred place in the village, the temple of Lord Shiva. It's small but very old. You must climb up the hill to reach there. It's mostly deserted during the daytime but all the children and elders frequent it at dusk. There is a puja held every day after sunset. It's very beautiful you should see it sometime", he smiled, his eyes shimmering from the dusty worn-out spectacles that he wore.

While sipping the sweet but strong and refreshing tea, I stared continuously at the temple. Somewhere something was stirring within my heart. "Hey, we have to reach Nagpur by the evening, and we just have around two hours of the journey left. That means we have around four hours still at our disposal. What say we go and have a look at the temple? The view of the village should be good from there. Maybe you could get some good 'Rural India' snaps from there", I offered. My friend smiled, not much of a pious person, he knew I had tugged him at the right place when I mentioned photography.

When we reached the bottom of the hillock, it turned out to be higher than our expectations. But we were now already committed to some action. My friend remarked, "The sun's pretty strong and there don't seem to be too many trees on the way up, we are going to be dead tired when we reach back". "It's okay man, we anyways have to sleep the entire day tomorrow. What else will we do in a house bustling with strangers coming for the marriage function?". "Why wouldn't we have a special appearance in the ladies sangeet?", he winked as we started uphill.

It was a steep, curvy climb, mostly in the open. Trees and shades were far and scattered. I realized it was indeed going to take some effort. No wonder the temple kept deserted in the afternoons. Fifteen minutes into the climb and we were panting. The urban lifestyle had done us in. We found a little shade under a young sparse tree and sat beneath it. My friend pulled out a water bottle from his knapsack and drank almost all of it. I managed with the remaining, choosing not to touch the one I had with me, as I knew we still had some way to go. None of us spoke, we both focused on the silence around us. For city dwellers like us, this was music. Now and then amongst the whirling wind, we could hear a bird tweet and the temple bells ring. As I pulled out a pack of fruits from my backpack, we saw a little girl, treading up the path, climbing her way rather hastily. She was wearing a school uniform and carried a few flowers and a tumbler of water in her hands. She was sweating and panting profusely as she passed by swiftly, probably on her way to the temple. By the time I finished helping myself to a ripe banana, she was out of sight.

We took two more breaks before we reached the top in about thirty more minutes. We realized how weak we had become sitting around the entire day in our chairs in the comfortable confines of our offices. The top of the hill was barren except the area surrounding the temple, which had a small garden attached to it. The view of the village from up above was spectacular. Tired to the core, we headed straight for the stairs of the temple to sit and relax a bit.

As we settled on the stairs under the shade of a small tree, I glanced around taking in the view. The temple seemed to be old, but not as old as the tea stall owner had promoted. Pre-independence maybe, I guessed, built under some Indian ruler. The garden was well done and it was nice to see it green and blossoming, defying the scorching sun which had otherwise dried up pretty much all the other vegetation around. I spotted the little girl, whom we had met on the way, kneeling, and praying in front of Lord Shiva's idol inside the temple. I smiled at her sincerity to brave the sun and climb all the way up for her prayers. My friend had gotten up and was greedily capturing his 'Rural India' photographs as if a famished person had been given a full course meal.

I wondered about the temple. The little girl was seen everywhere, busy as a bee, chiming bells, lighting incenses in front of the idols, offering water to the statues, and doing the rounds of the sacred basil plant. I was wonderstruck by her dedication. I had never seen such a dedicated worshipper in my life, at least not this young.

I spotted the temple priest and went to him to gather some information about the temple. He was an old wizened man. He was not sure about the history but was certain that it was built by the ruler of the place under British times and that his father and grandfather had served as the temple priests before him. As we were chatting, the little girl came up to the priest and said "My matchsticks have finished, could you please light this camphor stick for me". The priest told her to go search the matchsticks around the Ganesha idol, rather rudely, or so I comprehended. I watched as the girl quickly got hold of what she wanted and went back to being busy with her rituals. "What a sincere and cultured child", I remarked. The priest nodded his head. "Oh yes, very sincere girl, and very intelligent too. Her name is Chandani". "Looks like she's a regular. It must take a lot of courage and perseverance to come up all alone to this place in this scorching sun", I remarked. "Well yes, she comes here daily at this time, straight from the school, without fail, in good weather or bad, in sun or rain". I looked at the priest in marvel. "Is that true? Is she such a devout?". "Well, she has no choice! She's an inauspicious child. Of course, she wasn't so pious earlier. Last year she had gone to the Kumbh festival in Nashik with her parents. A stampede occurred there and thousands died and some went missing. She was separated from her parents in the melee and got rescued. Some good samaritans brought her back to the village. From the beginning, her father didn't like the kid very much. He was always beating and scolding her. He had always wanted a boy to work with him in the fields. Her mother had come up to me to look for a solution to this situation. The Kumbh was arriving and I thought it apt that they go and take a bath in the holy river as a family to develop a better bonding. However, god willed otherwise and the opposite happened. The village declared her as inauspicious, how could something such weird happen when they had gone for such a good cause. Anyways her parents have not returned yet".

"So, they died in the stampede?". "That lord Shiva only knows", replied the old man. "But if they would have been alive, they would have surely returned by now. They must be dead", I reasoned. "Please do not comment on what you do not know", he advised almost growling. "Chandani's grandmother brought her to me, weeping, and requested me to do something about her inauspiciousness. I had a look at her horoscope and suggested that if she performed these rituals daily at this temple for two years, she would get her parents back. You see she still has the yog in her horoscope which indicates the support of her parents in her life".

"What rubbish", I uttered unable to control my anger. "You know, sir, as well as I do how much time it takes for two adults to get back home after a mishap. Even if they were not healthy, or met some accident and were still alive, someone would be able to bring them home, like they did the little child. The poor girl is coming up here daily risking her health in this scorching sun performing rituals for something she will never get. Wouldn't it be a lot easier if she and everyone else accepted the bitter truth?" I said seething in resentment.

"What truth?" the priest demanded angrily. "That her parents are dead. That her hopes are misplaced and that the sooner she starts depending on herself, the better it is for her", I tried to reason. "How can I tell her a lie? It's all written in her horoscope that she will be continuously bestowed with parental love till she's married", the wizened man replied.

"So didn't you also see and predict the exact time when her parents will walk in. I would want to be around to welcome", I scoffed.

"My child", the priest said calmly, "you educated people don't know much, living in cities. We can't predict everything. We can just interpret. I merely suggested a way to get back what she wants. It's her grandmother who forces her to do this each day, else she might be thrown out of the house. So why don't you go and tell her all this educated stuff? Besides if she's inauspicious to her family it will do her good if she bows to the lord daily to ask for his forgiveness. If it would not have been for that village school teacher who's letting her study for free, her grandmother would have thrown her out anyway by now".

"I would have talked to her grandmother to answer your question, but I am sure she would be as stubborn, considering what she's making this poor child go through. As for that teacher, I am sure those are the type of people the village needs". I felt my friend, who had stopped his photography listening to the heated exchange, gently tugging me from behind.

I knew what he meant. I felt like an idiot to be reasoning with the man who stood in front of me, defiant, as if he was the almighty himself. Maybe he was for the village. Maybe they believed in his words more than they did in their conscience or the lord himself. I mellowed down, went inside the temple, bowed in front of the lord, said a little prayer, and walked out.

The little girl was now resting under a tree, searching for something in the sky and massaging her rough feet. I looked at her with a heavy heart and felt miserable and helpless. I wanted to tell her many things. I wanted to tell her that life is a struggle, where you don't always get what you want. I wanted to tell her that knowing the truth and accepting it makes one strong. That destiny is not written somewhere but made day after day by your thoughts, your actions. That the Lord is pleased by purity in thoughts and actions, by good deeds to oneself and others, rather than some of these unrealistic rituals. I wanted to tell her this and much more. But as I walked up to her, pulling out an apple from my backpack which I handed to her, my throat choked. All I could say was, "Chandani, be a brave girl".

10

QUAGMIRE

He puffed heavily on the cigarette in his hand and gazed absent-mindedly towards the horizon. The sun had begun its homeward journey to meet the golden sea that lay before the young man's eyes. A gentle breeze caressed his body. The scene was picturesque, the atmosphere balmy.

He sat there, smoking cigarette after cigarette, alone, aloof, indifferent to his surroundings. His mind was a beehive of confusing thoughts about past, present, and future. His heart was a seething cauldron of grief, too occupied with its problems to appreciate the natural beauty around. And his soul, it was tired. Tired of the incessant pains of the ever-present problems, tired of toil and sweat, of grief and loneliness. Tired perhaps of living!

A burning sensation connected him back to his immediate surroundings. He tossed the cigarette butt and drew out another from a pack in his pocket. For the umpteenth time in the day, he thought, "I surely couldn't have dropped it. It must be mom! She must've removed the matchbox from my trouser pockets". He nodded at his thought as if confirming his belief by his actions. He looked around to find someone with a light.

His search ended on the bench just adjacent to his where a couple was sitting, deeply engrossed in their flights of fantasy. He hated to disturb them but couldn't think of going any further to light up his stick. He politely asked the man, who was smoking himself, to give him a light. The man, seeing a decent-looking, neatly clad youngster in front of him, obliged happily.

Back on his bench, he coughed loudly, to relieve the congestion building up in his throat. He remembered how heavily he had been smoking for the past few months. He also recalled how worried his parents had been with his newly acquired habit, which had grown from a mere tranquilizer for frustration to an addiction, crossing the limits of college and entering home. His father had reasoned once or twice but couldn't convince him. He couldn't push an order down his throat for fear of having to face the consequences of snubbing a grown-up son. Poor mother, she always implored him to quit and he out of his sheer love for his mother, had always complied for some time. However once on his own, alone with his troubles and frustrations, he was always tempted into taking its refuge. Smoking made him forget the innumerous worries that life had thrown upon him.

The sun was now a deep red ball floating in the vast ocean that lay ahead. The breeze was steadily strong.

He continued puffing his newly lit cigarette vigorously as if punishing himself. His head was spinning. Too many thoughts cluttered his mind. He had been experiencing this trauma for the past, God knew – so many days. He needed rest, he had concluded, complete rest. But could anyone do that, rest completely, in today's reckless and worry-infested world.

He had considered taking a break, going on a holiday, but immediately his family's financial condition had blocked his train of thoughts. And so, he lived on with his problems, as do all, which grew day by day like a malignant tumour, giving him pangs of loneliness and frustration.

The wind picked up the pace and stole away a paper that was peeping out of his shirt pocket. On an impulse, he got up to go after it but changed his mind midway. He slumped back on the bench and saw the paper flutter on and on, assisted by the wind.

Then suddenly, it glided low and was caught under the foot of a passing vendor selling assorted nuts, and got crumpled.

He took his eyes off it and smiled sardonically. Another of those damned regret letters from employers whom he kept pursuing for a job.

He felt a rage bubbling inside, which he so often experienced, against the whole system, but could do nothing about. He knew he had wasted his entire youth in trying to achieve something, anything. He knew he was confused about what he wanted to do, what he was interested in doing. But he also knew that he was not alone. He had felt, seen, been privy to most youngsters of his age being in the same situation, running the rat race, succumbing to the pressures of the family, the society, its schools, and colleges. In his view fixed mindsets, insecurities, and short-sightedness prevalent amongst the last generation, never let the youth do what they were capable of!

His rage made him throw away the cigarette stick and cup his head in his palms as if to save it from blowing apart.

After a short while, he once again glanced around to find someone with a light. He intended to blow away every worry, every problem. He looked at the adjacent bench. The lovely couple had now moved to another bench to get more intimate. Unintentionally his eyes were caught by the bright and beautiful face of the girl. The wind played with her hair and her smile, which she flashed so often, seemed to light up the atmosphere around.

As much as he wanted to resist them, memories of Jaya invaded his heart and mind. He loathed to remember her at this moment and hence tore his eyes off the pretty girl whom he had been adoring. He gently shook his head and once again fumbled in his pocket to find a new cigarette. He now needed to light one badly, for a very painful chord had been struck in his heart. "A light, let's find a light"; he thought.

Back on his bench with his lit-up cigarette providing company, he spread his legs out and rested his head on the bench's shoulders, his eyes facing the vast arena above. The sun had bid its goodbye and the stars were slowly waking up, one by one. He gazed into the emptiness above and puffed releasing rings of smoke which rose, expanding, gliding, dancing and finally dissolving in the air. He watched them; he watched the sky. He couldn't resist thinking about Jaya, the girl he had so dearly loved, the girl who befriended him with all her charm, who used him shamelessly to gain the marks and the respect she wanted in college, coo-cooed paeans of love for him and then one day, when all was done, just walked away. She went away for higher studies to another city and never contacted him again. How he hated her! "Why am I even thinking about her"; he rose from the bench in anger and walked up to the parapet of the promenade by the sea, gazing down into the foaming blackness.

After a few minutes, he glanced at his watch, "My God! It's late, Ma must be waiting", he thought and started walking back towards the road. After a few steps though, he slowed down and then stopped. He remembered why he was at that place, at that time. He walked back towards the bench and sat down again. "Let her wait, she will have to get used to it after all". He felt his eyes getting moist. They had done so much for him; his family and he hadn't been able to give them anything back. He had always let them down, always been a source of worry for them. They loved him; he knew. The feeling was mutual. He felt sorry for them, especially for his sister. She was the person he loved most in the world. All his faults, failure, or foibles, never lessened her love for him. She had been his greatest pillar of strength till now. "Till now...", he thought and sighed.

He glanced at his watch. It was late. He looked around; the streets now wore a deserted look. Only a few people were present on a few benches but far away from him. He pulled himself up and walked up to the parapet of the promenade. The sea was now a raging cauldron of madness, its waves crashing against the parapet, waging a fierce battle with the walls.

He looked down and made a quick decision, he would smoke one last time. He took out the pack from his pocket and opened it. It was empty. He looked at it absent-mindedly and then laughed slightly in a strange, dull tone. His luck would never change. He really needed this last one to rest in peace. His eyes moistened as he climbed up the parapet wall, gazing at the abyss ahead. Slowly he dropped the empty cigarette case into the sea.

He watched it fall, slowly into the vastness beneath. He looked around, there was no one nearby. The darkness ahead beckoned him, promising eternal bliss. The sea waves crashed on the walls of the promenade, shrieking in anger. The wind howled in his ears, singing a mournful song. The time had come. He closed his eyes. He could feel his mother calling for dinner. He could feel his sister glancing at the clock, waiting for him. He could visualize his father laying the chessboard patiently, for their daily match. Tears trickled from his eyes unabashedly as he felt a surge of emotions. He felt the sea lure him towards itself but the wind pushing him away from the parapet in the opposite direction. And while the elements tussled with each other he suddenly heard a familiar sound in the distance. The honking of a bus horn. He opened his eyes and glanced around. A red city transport bus was standing on the bus stand that was visible from afar. Closer to him he saw a weathered man in his forties walking up to him. The man wore a khaki uniform and carried a bag around his shoulder. He recognized the man instantly; it was the conductor of the bus he took home every day from here or somewhere down the route.

He glanced at his watch. "Strange, they are ten minutes early today". The conductor read his mind. "Well yes, a bit early today, aren't we?", the conductor smiled as he approached near and climbed up the parapet to stand near the young man. "That's life, you reach early somewhere, and at other places much later. Bad traffic jam on some days, clear roads on another! A deluge of passengers on most days and dearth of passengers such as today! All moving variables in our job, you see. But all these years into this service one thing is certain young man, we do reach where we want to eventually". By now, the conductor was up on the parapet, stretching his arms and taking in the fresh air. "The driver drove well today, so we decided to take a quick breather here. No passengers yet on the bus, so we had the liberty. Besides we knew you would be somewhere here waiting for the bus". The conductor pulled out a pack of cigarettes from his pocket and helped himself to one. "I can only do this off duty, I need this one really bad today". "Why?", the young man asked feebly. The conductor looked at him, melancholy in his eyes. "Well, today is my daughter's birthday". The conductor waved the pack to the young man offering him one. He eagerly accepted. "That's great", said the young man, puzzled about what the conductor was so forlorn about. "Yes, just that she's not around to enjoy it. We lost her five years back in a fatal road accident. Bright young mind she was".

They smoked in silence for the next few minutes, puffing and gazing at the dark waters of the sea. And then they heard the horn again, once, twice. "Work beckons. Life must go on my friend", the conductor smiled. "Come, let's get you home!".

They climbed down the parapet and started walking slowly back towards the waiting bus.

11

THE LAND OF GOLDEN DUNES

Thar- the desert, a land of golden sand dunes and beautiful sunsets, a land teeming with folklores of bravery and romance, a land resounding with haunting folk melodies and soul-stirring ballads. It's a tourist's treat, a nature lovers paradise. But at the same time, it's an abyss of misery for local inhabitants, who live on through thick and thin wearing a smile on their faces, braving the atrocities of the elements but still proud of their great heritage. It was in this vast desert that a great number of days of my early life were spent.

Although we were settled in Jaipur during those days, most of the time I was travelling and camping with my father thanks to his profession. He was a Geologist. Since I hadn't started formal schooling at that age, accompanying my father was not a challenge. Even when my schooling did start, my father made it sure that he took us all along during the holidays.

My father's camping locations ranged from the exteriors of small towns around Thar to villages in the middle of the desert. A few workers and drivers (for the official vehicles) always accompanied us. On arrival at the camping site, the hunt for a dwelling would begin. If luck favoured, we would find a decadent dak-bungalow or a former government establishment. But often we landed up raising tents which would be our dwelling place for the next few months.

A couple of days later a few laborers from the nearby villagers would be contracted and then began my father's work, leaving me and my mother free to have a stroll in our endless backyard. The intolerable heat did not give us much chance to see things around during day time. So, we remained confined to our tents passing time by playing board games, listening to the radio, reading books, or simply taking cat naps. Without electric fans, the afternoons in the simmering desert were no less than hell. Our only steadfast friends in that heat were mats made of khus grass that were sprinkled with water now and then to provide a cool environment around. An occasional table fan in some of the camps was no more than a miracle.

But if days were hell, evenings were heaven. Each day I waited anxiously for the sun to go down beneath the tiny dunes heralding the approach of freedom. It was in the evenings that I would be let out in the open. It was in the evenings that I would run and climb up to the tiny dunes around and wave to mother from there. It was in the evenings that father and I walked up to the nearby canals and sat together looking at the calm waters.

Evenings were real fun and each evening held a new fascination.

As the evening died and the pall of darkness fell over the desert, we once again confined ourselves to our haven. Although the pale moonlight made the desert look no less than a fairyland yet the mystic darkness and dead calm all around made me prefer the safety of the electric lamp which we had inside our tents. As the night wore on, snakes and scorpions, the size of whom left us aghast, surfaced near our tents. The innumerous encounters with these lethal creatures soon became an order of the day (rather night!).

However, our alert night guards, assisted by the ever-friendly dogs around, made sure that no harm came our way.

To add to our woes, devastating sand storms, so common in the desert, often invaded us at night and threw the entire camp out of gear. We stayed up for hours during those storms, each of us clinging to the ropes and poles of our tents, which would otherwise be uprooted by the sheer power of the storm, praying for it to pass away soon. When it did, we once again stretched ourselves on the cots only to be woken up minutes later by another hissing sound.

No doubt life in the Thar was harsh and hard, yet I enjoyed those days immensely. There was something very rustic, very adventurous about those experiences that we had staying in a desert. The memories of those days are still treasured in my heart. Nostalgic visions of those beautiful sunsets, the still, ageless golden dunes, those placid waters of the canal, those tinkling of bells from the camel caravans passing by, and the impressions left by my small feet on the sands of the Thar, are too precious to forget!

12

Sleeping with Count Dracula

It's midnight. You lie down on your bed surrendering to your drooping eyelids. A good night's sleep is all that you want. Soon you are transported to another world. Huge mountains, valleys teeming with flowers, flying horses, talking birds, dancing girls, everything is so breath-taking. Suddenly you hear a distant buzzing sound. "A helicopter perhaps", you think, but the idea of a machine in this part of the world seems alien. The noise escalates. The birds run amok and horses fly away. The mountains start crumbling and your vision gets blurred. Then, suddenly, there is the sound of a slap followed by a shrill note as if someone is tuning a microphone. You return to your senses with a jolt and everything becomes crystal clear. The helicopter was a cursed mosquito and you had evidently slapped your ears, a natural reflex, to catch hold of it. Obviously, the culprit had already escaped.

This is a common story in a household plagued by these terrors on wings. A peaceful sleep can be easily ruined by these worthless, omnipresent, odious microcosms of Count Dracula, continuously pricking your skins with their built-in straws to have their favourite drink. And before you react, they are gone with the wind (read win) leaving you doing dumb things like slapping your face or scratching your own body madly to alleviate the itching.

One may argue that with the advent of innumerous mosquito eliminating gadgets it's hard to believe that such a small creature can terrorize a person so much. To that, I would reply that there is a thing called "adaptability" of which this creature is the best paradigm.

Your Good Night and All Out would work fine for a few days but soon the situation would be back to square one.

Summers may find you in deep slumber without much interruption. The air from the powerful fans and coolers, assisted by the mosquito repellent devices greatly impairs the radar systems of these devils in disguise, making them fly like feathers in a storm. But the tables turn in winters. The fans are dead and your sleekly designed repellent machines fail very soon, leaving you on the battlefield, along with the enemy. You cover your body with blankets and bedsheets but the shrewd crooks find their way in somehow. And then begins an unending saga of misery. The guerrilla warriors bite you here and there, shattering your sweet dreams. Still dozing, your mind guides and hand traces the victimized spot. And then you scratch away to glory ultimately shattering your sleep.

This repeats itself throughout the night, till your senses give way and you succumb to the creature's attacks.

However, where the modern gadgets fail, your old ally, the mosquito net, comes to your rescue. Agreed that the idea seems a bit uncomfortable and superannuated but I would like to emphasize that nothing comes close to this if you do not want to become a victim of malaria. However, caution is the key here. I have myself empirically perfected the art of mosquito net management and disclose it to you, my dear reader, free of charge.

Put on the net over the bed, hung from the side by strings nailed to the walls, or by the more expensive method of putting them over rods attached to your bed. Carefully tuck in the sides of the mosquito net under the mattress and get rid of your foes. Sounds simple right! Well now for the catch! You must be careful not to allow any of these demons to enter your haven when you are deploying the net or while stepping in or out of the safe zone. Even a single enemy warrior inside the net can ruin your night's peace.

But we are humans and hence a few slippages are likely to happen.

Here, I would like to introduce you to the "Frog Leap" and "Tiger's Prey" methods devised by me to eliminate any mosquitoes which might have crept in due to our negligence.

The former consists of killing the mosquito in mid-air. Take a convenient position on the bed, inside the mosquito net, and trace down your enemy. Shake the net slightly if the mosquito is resting on the walls of the net, to make it fly. All set now leap forward imitating a frog as best as you can and clap to kill the foe between your palms, in mid-air.

Imagining yourself executing the famous dives of your favourite action heroes should help here. Do not leap too high or too fast which may result in a crash landing and (god forbid) broken bones.

The second method, Tigers Prey, gets its name from the idiosyncrasy of a tiger to keenly observe its prey and strike suddenly. Here, after you have confirmed the presence of an enemy warrior inside your net, move stealthily towards it slowly bringing your palms near it. When close enough, clap with vengeance, grabbing and squeezing the mosquito on the sides of the net itself.

It's very understandable if you get too involved in these antics and their rehearsals for attaining perfection. However, it's my duty to add a note of caution here. While performing these tricks amateurs are advised to lock the doors and windows of their room as they are likely to make a lot of queer noises and perform rare visual feats that are likely to give any peeping neighbours long-lasting fits of laughter!

Before retiring to the bed finally for the day be careful not to let the enemy in when you go out to switch off the light. Beginners are advised to drag their beds near a light switch so that they can reach for it from within the net thereby precluding chances of a security lapse (never mind the loud noise generated while dragging it, precaution is better than cure they say).

All said and done now is the time to reap the rewards of your hard work. Without further ado hit the bed and close your eyes and let yourself be transported to a world where the sights are truly sumptuous.

What can be explained is not poetry

- William Butler Yeats

Poems

1

REVIVAL

After a long, dreadful storm,
From the distant horizon,
Break the first rays of the sun,
Warm and sparkling,
Heralding a new day,
Infusing a new strength,
Conveying a message,
To live on through the tides,
And cherish life, in all ups and downs.
Radiating hope, for a better tomorrow,
Away from the haunting visions of yesterday,
Towards an inviting future,
That has in store,
All of life's precious pearls.

2

WHISPERING ANGELS

I hear the angels whisper,
When starving babies cry,
I hear them call out,
When people fight and die.

When the lovely dove of peace,
Is shot down by humanity,
When havoc prevails everywhere,
Due to man's insanity.

When the pure stream of human nature,
Loses its flow and way,
"This was not God's will",
I hear the angels say.

But when the sun is shining,
And birds are flying in the sky,
And down on earth, two humans,
Embrace each other in joy.

When contentment, happiness, and peace,
Prevail on land and sea,
I hear the angels whisper,
"O God, let this forever be!"

3

THE TRYST

A little bird, sat on the branch,
Of a barren tree, lonely, still,
Gazing into infinity, constantly,
Never hopping, never fluttering,
Never tweeting, never chattering.
Just once in a long while, it moved slightly,
Lifting a wing,
Or what was left of it,
Ever so slowly, almost painfully,
And gently hugged it back again,
Never letting its eyes end,
Their tryst with the blue sky.

I watched it sitting tirelessly,
Through the window for long,
I felt the pain return,
And limped back to the bed,
A nurse helped me get in,
Administered some pills and left.

Gazing out of the window again,
I found the sun dying slowly,
The little bird still sat there,
On the branch of that barren tree,
Gazing into the vastness ahead,
And telling it,
A never-ending story!

4

THE ROAD AHEAD

Move on, march along,
The way is clear,
See ahead, don't look back,
Your goal is very near.

Raise high your spirits,
Flash your charming smile,
Have faith and courage,
Destination is another mile.

Think not of losing,
For it really matters not,
Just move, keep going,
Give it your best shot.

March through ups and downs,
Forget your frustrations,
Time will surely see you,
Reach your destination.

5

THE CALL OF KASHI

Time and again,
I hear it call,
The river beckons me,
The city beckons.

Without a rhyme or reason,
Over matter sometimes trivial,
I visit the city frequently,
For me, it's a puzzle.

It's not my birthplace,
It's not my home,
And yet it calls me,
In happiness and gloom.

The love of its people,
The bells of the temples,
Have something to do,
With this strange connection.

This is a tryst,
With roots in the unknown,
There is a purpose, a message,
When the city beckons.

Even when I am miles away,
In my heart, I know,
Another reason, another trip,
Another call's not far away.

6

Do We Care?

Nature has been wounded,
Thousands dead,
Unrest prevails,
People are vexed,
Love is lost,
Peace is no more,
Wars wreak havoc,
Crime and violence soar.
Our life, our planet, our existence,
All's at stake,
But do we care,
Do we really care?

7

A WORLD WITHOUT YOU

No moon in the sky,
Nor any stars,
No light in my life,
The nights are dark.

All hopes are lost,
My future is bleak,
My world is a void,
I feel so weak.

The sun shines no more,
The winds don't blow,
No birds chirp for me,
Life has lost its glow.

I close my eyes,
And find you there,
In a beautiful world,
A world without despair.

I reopen them,
The sorrows return,
Oh, how I wish,
That you could learn,

How alone I am,
In this world.

8

THE COMMON MAN

He sat in a corner,
The poor, common man,
Clothes torn, ribs protruding,
His sunken, vexed eyes, staring;
Men in Khadi, around him,
Greed on their faces.
"Relax, my man,
We've only just come for your vote".
"Politicians!" he shudders,
"They are here again!"

The man in saffron initiates,
"Give me your vote,
And I shall give you a temple!"
The elder with the topi next,
"Come with me,
Expand, Privatize, Globalize,
Celebrate the 21st century",
"They are all liars, support me;
I promise a separate state,
A land of freedom"; roars the bearded,

"Caste, Community, Reservations",
Others join in,
Leaving the man puzzled.
Feebly he speaks,
"Who gives me food, clothes, dwelling?
How about a job,
Did I hear security?
Peace and prosperity?"
He glances around,
Looking at them in anticipation.

"Naïve, unprogressive, atheist ...",
They mutter and retreat.
"Hold a rally", "Stage a dharna",
"Fix him up", "Incite the mob",
Their voices fade in the distance.
"Father who were they?", asks his son,
Sitting beside him in awe,
The common man sighs,
"My son, if you must know,
They are the rulers of our nation!"

9

Death

She knocks at the door,
To let her in,
I ignore her calls,
Can't let her win.

She wants to enter,
Many doubts I make,
There's hope, it's not time yet,
Surely, it's some mistake.

But she listens not to me,
And throws open the door,
Cruelly she snatches him away,
Heavenwards they soar.

And while we're crying and grieving,
She casts a helpless last look,
" Nothing I can do about it,
It's in the almighty's rule book".

10

MAN AND GOD

He was born untimely,
He came in this world,
Defying all laws of nature,
He learned and grew,
Wisdom dawned on him,
And he clearly knew,
That man was one,
That together they made the world,
That boundaries of distinction,
Are a trivial issue.
He spoke out his opinion,
Tyrants cried him down,
No one believed him.
He continued to preach,
To convey his message of love and unity,
But people, ignorant people, wouldn't listen.
Till one day,
When havoc struck earth,
Thousands were doomed,
Except the few who stood by him.
Then man learnt,
How right he was,

That he was above ordinary,
A miracle, an enigma,
An eternal entity,
Who spoke the truth,
And cared for humanity.
Thereafter generations to follow,
Took to his teachings,
And one fine day,
They gave him a name,
They called him God.

11

THE UNCERTAIN STORY

The trauma is intense,
The mind, confused,
The soul is anxious,
The state, stewed.

The road ahead's uncertain,
The darkness, ominous,
The troubles are many,
The hurdles, voluminous.

The goal is far away,
The distance, unknown,
The hope's mingled with vanity,
The effort is his alone.

The outcome is dubious,
The time will tell it all,
The wishes are with him,
Will destiny see him being extolled?

12

THE SAND DUNES

They glitter like gold in the rays of the sun,
The sand dunes, shimmering and bright,
They're small, they're big, the pride of the desert,
And they present a beautiful sight.

They're the offspring of the golden dust,
The friends of wind and light,
The desert is their dwelling place,
Where all is still and quiet.

They rest and sleep in the desert,
The sand dunes are a peaceful lot,
But when they lose their temper,
They destroy whatever they spot.

Since ages, they've stood in the desert,
Watching the time pass by,
They grow, they shift, they travel,
But the sand dunes never die.

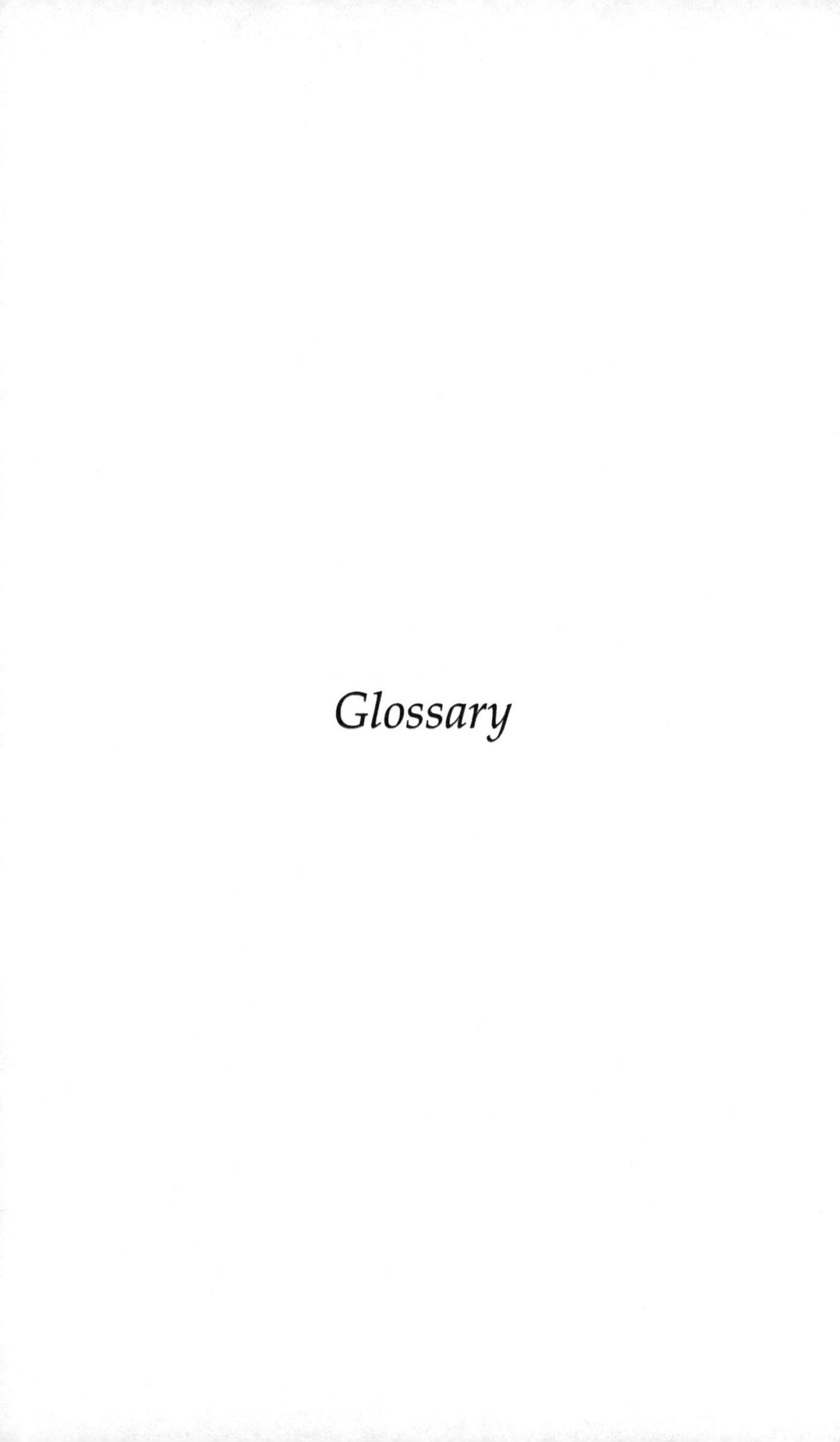

Glossary

Arsa – A local sweet from the hilly state of Uttarakhand.

Bal Mithai – A popular brown sweet, coated with white sugar balls, from the Himalayan state of Uttarakhand.

Beedi – a type of cheap strong cigarette made from tobacco rolled in tendu leaf.

Bhaat – Steamed sticky rice.

Bhai – (Literally) Brother, used in many parts of India as a suffix to the name, to show respect.

Bhaiya – (Literally) Brother, used in many parts of India as a suffix to the name or a substitute to address someone unknown with respect.

Bhoot bangla- Haunted house.

Chacha – Uncle.

Dharna – a protest, to reflect disagreement with something, by refusing to leave a place.

Ji – Used as a suffix to the name to show respect, especially someone elder.

Keema Pav – A popular street food in India made of minced meat (Keema) and served with local bread(Pav).

Khichdi – A household Indian dish made of rice and lentils, gentle on stomach.

Laata – 'Idiot' in local language in the hilly state of Uttarakhand.

Nullah – A big watercourse usually for drainage.

Oija – Similar to 'Oh my god' in local language in the hilly state of Uttarakhand.

Pujari – Priest

Shahzaada – Prince

Singori – Another local delicacy from the hilly state of Uttarakhand.

Ustad – Literally master or expert, but also used as a suffix to names for mentors.

Yog – (here) Indication, chance of happening, meeting